Richard Dowling

The Weird Sisters

Vol. 1

Richard Dowling

The Weird Sisters
Vol. 1

ISBN/EAN: 9783337054496

Printed in Europe, USA, Canada, Australia, Japan

Cover: Foto ©Andreas Hilbeck / pixelio.de

More available books at **www.hansebooks.com**

THE WEIRD SISTERS.

A Romance.

BY

RICHARD DOWLING,

AUTHOR OF "THE MYSTERY OF KILLARD."

In Three Volumes.

VOL. I.

LONDON:

TINSLEY BROTHERS, 8, CATHERINE ST., STRAND.

1880.

EDMOND POWER, ESQ.,

OF SPRINGFIELD,

𝔚hose kindness to 𝔐ine and to 𝔐e

I SHALL NEVER FORGET

WHILE I AM.

CONTENTS.

Part I.—A Plain Gold Guard.

THE WEIRD SISTERS.

PART I. A PLAIN GOLD GUARD.

CHAPTER I.

A CONSCIENTIOUS BURGLAR.

Mr. Henry Walter Grey sat in his dining-room sipping claret on the evening of Monday, the 27th August, 1866. His house was in the suburbs of the city of Daneford.

Mr. Grey was a man of about forty-five years of age, looking no more than thirty-eight. He was tall, broad, without the least tendency to corpulency, and yet pleasantly rounded and full. There was no angularity or harshness in his face or figure. The figure was active looking and powerful, the face open, joyous, and benignant. The hair had begun to thin at his forehead; this gave his face a soothing expression of contented calm.

His forehead was broad and white; his eyes were constant, candid, and kindly; his nose was large, with quickly-mobile sensitive nostrils; and his mouth well formed and full, having a sly uptwist at one corner, indicating strong sympathy with humour. He wore neither beard nor moustache.

His complexion was bright without being florid, fair without being white. His skin was smooth as a young girl's cheek. He stood six feet without his boots. He was this evening in the deepest mourning for his wife, whom he had lost on Friday, the 17th of that month, August.

Although he occupied one of the most important positions in Daneford, no person who knew him, or had heard of him from a Danefordian, ever called him either Henry or Walter. He was universally known as Wat Grey. Daneford believed him to be enormously rich. He was the owner of the Daneford Bank, an institution which did a large business and held its head high.

Indeed, in Daneford it was almost unnecesssary to add the banker's surname to his Christian name; and if anyone said, "Wat did so-and-so," and you asked, "Wat who?" the purveyor of the news would know you for an alien or a nobody in the city.

The young men worshipped him as one of themselves, who, despite his gaiety and lightheartedness, had prospered in the world, and kept his youth and made his money, and was one of themselves still, and would continue to be one of them as long as he lived.

Elder men liked him for the solid

prudence which guided all his business transactions, and which, while it enabled him to be with the young, allowed him to exercise over his juniors in years the influence of an equal combined with the authority of experience. Lads of twenty never thought of him as a fogey, and men of thirty looked upon him as a younger man, who had learned the folly of vicious vanities very much sooner than others; and consequently they confided in him, and submitted themselves to him with docility. Young men assembled at his house, but there were no orgies; elder men came, and went away cheered and diverted, and no whit the less rich or wise because discussions of important matters had been enlivened with interludes of gayer discourse.

Wat Grey was one of the most active men in Daneford. He was Chairman of the Chamber of Commerce, of

the Commercial Club, and of the
Harbour Board.

He was Vice-chairman of the Daneford
Boat Club, and Treasurer of the Poor's
Christmas Coal Fund.

If he was rich, he was liberal. He
subscribed splendidly to all the local
charities, but never as a public man or
as owner of the Daneford Bank. What
he thought it wise to give he always
sent from "Wat," as though he prized
more highly the distinction of familiarity
his town had conferred upon him than
any conventional array of Christian and
surnames, or any title of cold courtesy
or routine right. It was not often
he dropped from his cheerful level of
high-spirited and rich animal enjoyment
into sentimentalism, but on one occasion
he said to young Feltoe: "I'd rather be
'Wat' to my friends than Sir Thingumbob
Giggamarigs to all the rest of the world."

There was nothing Daneford could have refused him. He had been mayor, and could be Liberal member of Parliament for the ancient and small constituency any time he chose when the Liberal seat was vacant. Daneford was one of those constituencies which give one hand to one side and the other hand to the other, and have no hand free for action. Walter Grey had always declined the seat; he would say:

"I'm too young yet, far too young. As I grow older, I shall grow wiser and more corrupt. Then you can put me in, and I shall have great pleasure in ratting for a baronetcy. Ha, ha, ha!"

Of late, however, it had been rumoured the chance of getting the rich banker to consent to take the seat (this was the way everyone put it) had increased, and that he might be induced to stand at the next vacancy. Then all who knew of his personal qualities, his immense knowledge of finance, and his large fortune, said that if he chose he might be Chancellor of the Exchequer in time ; and after his retirement from business, and purchase of an estate, the refusal of a peerage was certain to come his way.

As he sat sipping his claret that Monday evening of the 27th of August, 1866, his face was as placid as a secret well. Whether he was thinking of his dead wife and sorrowing for her, or revolving the ordinary matters of his banking business, or devising some scheme for the reduction of taxation in the city, or dallying mentally with the sirens who sought to ensnare him in parliamentary honours, could no more be gathered from his face than from the dull heavy clouds that hung low over the sultry land abroad.

It was not often he had to smoke his after-dinner cigar and sip his after-dinner

claret alone; men were always glad to dine
with him, and he was always glad to have
them; but the newness of his black clothes
and of the bands on his hats in the hall
accounted for the absence of guests. He
was not dressed for dinner. One of the
things which had made his table so free
and jovial was that a man might sit down
to it in a coat of any cut or colour, and
in top-boots and breeches if he liked.
Before his bereavement he would say:

"Mrs. Grey—although she may not sit
with us—has an antiquated objection to
a man dining in his shirt-sleeves. I have
often expostulated with her unreasonable
prejudice, but I can't get her to concede
no coat at all You may wear your hat
and your gloves if you like, but for
Heaven's sake come in a coat of some kind.
If you can't manage a coat, a jacket will
do splendidly."

Mrs. Grey never dined out. In fact,

she saw little company; tea was always sent into the dining-room.

Mr. Grey had not got more than half-way through his cigar on that evening of the 27th of August when a servant knocked and entered.

The master, whose face was towards the window, turned round his head slowly, and said in a kindly voice:

"Well, James, what is it?"

"A man, sir, wants to see you."

James was thick-set, low-sized, near-sighted, and dull. He had been a private soldier in a foot regiment, and had been obliged to leave because of his increasing near-sightedness. But he had been long enough in uniform to acquire the accomplishment of strict and literal attention to orders, and the complete suspension of his own faculties of judgment and discretion. Although his master was several inches taller than James, the latter

looked in the presence of the banker like
a clumsy elephant beside an elegant
panther.

"A man wants to see me!" cried Mr.
Grey, in astonishment, not unmixed with
a sense of the ridiculous. "What kind
of a man? and what is his business."

He glanced good-humouredly at James,
but owing to the shortness of the servant's
sight the expression of the master's face
was wasted in air.

James, who had but a small stock of
observation and no fancy, replied respectfully :

"He seems a common man, sir; like
a man you'd see in the street."

"Ah," said Mr. Grey, with a smile ;
"that sort of man, is it? Ah! Which,
James, do you mean : the sort of man
you'd see walking in the streets, or
standing at a public-house corner?"

Again Mr. Grey smiled at the droll

dulness and droller simplicity of his servant.

A gleam of light came into James's dim eyes upon finding the description narrowed down to the selection of one of two characteristics, and he said, in a voice of solemn sagacity :

"The back of his coat is dirty, sir, as if he'd been leaning against a public-house wall."

"Or as if he had been carrying a sack of corn on his back?" demanded the master, laughing softly, and brushing imaginary cigar - ashes off the polished oak - table with his white curved little finger.

For a moment James stood on his heels in stupefied doubt and dismay at this close questioning. He was a man of action, not of thought. Had his master shouted, "Right wheel—quick march!" he would have gone out of the window, through the glass, without a murmur and without a thought of reproach; but to be thus interrogated on subtleties of appearance made him feel like a blindfold man, who is certain he is about to be attacked, but does not know where, by whom, or with what weapon. He resolved to risk all and escape.

"I think, sir, it was a public-house, for I smelt liquor."

"That is conclusive," said the master, laughing out at last. "That is all right, James. I am too lazy to go down to see him. Show him up here. Stop a moment, James. Let him come up in five minutes."

The servant left the room, and as he did so the master laughed still more loudly, and then chuckled softly to himself, muttering:

"He thought the man had been leaning against a public-house because he smelt

of liquor! Ha, ha, ha! My quaint
James, you will be the death of your
master. You will, indeed."

When he had finished his laugh he
dismissed the idea of James finally with
a roguish shrug of his shoulders and wag
of his head.

Then he drew down the gasalier,
pushed an enormous easy-chair in front
of the empty fire-place, pulled a small
table between the dining-table and the
easy-chair, and placed an ordinary oak
and green dining-room chair at the corner
of the dining-table near the window;
then he sat down on the ordinary chair.

When this was done he ascertained
that the drawer of the small table opened
easily, closed in the drawer softly, threw
himself back in his own chair and began
smoking slowly, blowing the smoke towards
the ceiling without taking the cigar from
his lips, and keeping his legs thrust out

before him, and his hands deep in his trousers-pockets.

Presently the door opened; James said, "The man, sir!" the door closed again, and all was still.

"Come over and sit down, my man," said the banker, in a good-natured tone of voice, without, however, removing his eyes from the ceiling.

To this there was no reply by either sound or gesture.

Mr. Grey must have been pursuing some humorous thought over the ceiling; for when he at last dropped his eyes and looked towards the door, he said, with a quiet sigh, as though the ridiculous in the world was killing him slowly: "It's too droll, too droll." Then to the man, who still stood just inside the door: "Come over here and sit down, my man. I have been expecting a call from you. Come over and sit down. Or would you prefer I should send the brougham for you ?"

As he turned his eyes round, they fell on the figure of a man of forty, who, with head depressed and shoulders thrust up high, and a battered, worn sealskin-cap held in both hands close together, thumbs uppermost, was standing on one leg, a model of abject, obsequious servility.

The man made no reply ; but as Mr. Grey's eyes fell upon him he substituted the leg drawn up for the one on which he had been standing, thrust up his shoulders, and pressed down his head in token of unspeakable humility under the honour of Mr. Grey's glance, and of profound gratitude for the honour of Mr. Grey's speech.

" Come, my man ; do come over and sit down. The conversation is becoming monotonous already. Do come over, and sit down here. I can't keep on saying

'come' all the evening. I assure you I
have expected this call from you. Do
come and sit down."

Mr. Grey motioned the man to the
large easy-chair in front of him.

At last the man moved, stealthily,
furtively, across the carpet, skirting the
furniture cautiously, as though it consisted
of infernal-machines which might go off
at any moment. His dress was ragged
and torn; his face, a long narrow one,
of mahogany colour; his eyes were bright
full blue, the one good feature in his shy
unhandsome countenance.

" Sit in that chair," said Mr. Grey
blandly, at the same time waving his
hand towards the capacious and luxurious
easy-chair.

" Please, sir, I'd rather stand," said
the man, in a low sneaking tone.   *//*

The contrast between the two was
remarkably striking: the one, large and

liberal of aspect, gracious and humorous of manner, broad-faced, generous-looking, perfectly dressed, scrupulously neat; the other, drawn together, mean in form, narrow of features, with avaricious mouth and unsteady eye, with ragged and soiled clothes.

"Sit down, my good man; sit down. I assure you the conversation will continue to be very monotonous until you take my advice, and sit down in that chair. You need not be afraid of spoiling it. Sit down, and then you may at your leisure tell me what I can do for you."

Mr. Grey may have smiled at the whim of Nature in forging such a counter-feit of human nature as the man before him, or he may have smiled at the obvious dislike with which his visitor surveyed the chair. The smile, however, was a pleasant, cordial, happy one. He drew in his legs, sat upright, and, leaning his left

elbow on the small table before him,
pointed to the chair with his right hand,
and kept his right hand fixed in the at-
titude of pointing until the man, with a
scowl at the chair and a violent upheaval
of his shoulders and depression of his
head, sank among the soft cushions.

"Now we shall get on much more
comfortably," said Mr. Grey, placing what
remained unsmoked of his cigar on the
ash-tray beside him, clasping his hands
over his waistcoat, and bending slightly
forward to indicate that his best attention was at the disposal of his visitor.
"What is your name?"

"Joe Farleg."

"Joe Farleg, Joe Farleg," mused, half
aloud, Mr. Grey. "An odd name. Why
am I fated always to meet people with
odd ways or odd names? Well, never
mind answering that question, Joe," he
said, more loudly, in an indulgent tone,

as though he felt he would be violating
kindliness by insisting on a reply which
had little or nothing to do with Farleg.
He continued, " I don't think I have ever
seen you or heard your name before ;
and although I did not think it improbable
you, or someone like you, would call, I
could not know exactly whom I was to
see. Before we go any farther, I ask
you : Haven't I been good to you without
even knowing who you were ?"

" Good to me, sir !" cried the man,
in surprise.

" Yes ; I have been very good to you
in not setting the police after you."

The man tried to struggle up out of
the chair, but, unused to a seat of the
kind, struggled for a moment in vain.
At last he gained his feet, and with an
oath demanded : " How did you know I
did it ? Are you going to set them after
me now ?" His blue eyes swiftly explored

the room to find if the officers had sprung
out of concealment, and to ascertain the
chances of his escape.

With a kindly wave of his hand,
Mr. Grey indicated the chair. " I have
not even spoken to the police about the
matter, and I do not intend speaking to
them. Sit down in your chair, Joe, and
let us talk the matter over quietly."

" I'm d — d if I sit in that chair
again. It smothers me."

He regarded the banker with uneasiness and the chair with terror.

Mr. Grey laughed outright. The laughter seemed to soothe Farleg a little. He
cast his large blue eyes once more hastily
round the room, then regarded the banker
for an instant, and dropped his glance
upon the chair.

Nothing could have been more reassuring than the brilliantly-lighted dining-
room, the good-natured, good-humoured

face of its master, and the harmlessly
seductive appearance of the chair. Farleg
was ashamed of his fears; upon another
invitation, and an assurance that nothing
farther would be said by his host until
he had returned to his former position,
he threw himself once more into the
comfortable seat.

"And now, Joe, that we are in a
position to go on smoothly, what can I
do for you?"

"You remember, sir, the night of the
robbery, sir?"

"Yes; you broke into my house, into
one of the tower-rooms, on the evening
of the 17th of this month, and you carried
off a few things of no great value."

"And you're not going to send the
police after me?"

"No."

Farleg leaned forward in his chair
until his elbows rested on his knees.

"You missed the things. You said a while ago you expected me, or whoever did the robbery; was that a true word? Did you expect whoever did the robbery to come and see you?"

"I did. I could not be sure you would come, but when I missed the things I thought you might call. There was, of course, the chance you might not."

"That's it. Well, I have come, you see. I found some rings, and I kept three; but I thought you might like to have this one, and I brought it to you, as I am about to leave the country. Look at it. It's a plain gold guard."

As Farleg said these words his eyes, no longer wandering, fixed themselves on the face of Mr. Grey.

For an instant the face of the banker puckered and wrinkled up like a blighted leaf. Almost instantly it smoothed out again; and, with a bland smile, he said:

"Thank you very much. It was my poor wife's guard ring. You were very kind to think of bringing it back to me."

As he spoke he began softly opening the drawer of the little table that stood between him and the burglar.

CHAPTER II.

A GENEROUS BANKER.

THE ring lay on the little table. Mr. Grey did not take it up, but left it where Farleg had placed it.

When the banker had pulled out the drawer half-a-dozen inches, he looked up from the ring, and, with a glance of kindly interest, said:

"So you intend leaving the country. Why? And where do you purpose going?"

Farleg looked down at his boots, and thrust up his shoulders as he answered:

"Well, sir, things are getting hot, and the place is getting hot. It isn't every one has so much consideration as you

for a man who has to live as best he
can——"

" Poor fellow ! "

"And if I and the old woman don't
clear out of this soon, why, they'll be
sending me away, ' Carriage paid : with
care.' "

He paused, raised his head, and turned
those prominent blue eyes on the face of
the banker. The latter was drawing small
circles on the table in front of him with
the white forefinger of his left hand, his
eyes intently followed his finger, his
white right hand rested on the edge of
the partly open drawer.

Mr. Grey said, softly and emphatically :
" I understand, I understand. Go on, and
don't be afraid to speak plainly, Joe. May
I ask you what you were before you devoted yourself to your present—profession?
Your conversation and way of putting
things are far above the average of men

of your calling;" with a smile of sly interest.

"I was a clerk, sir," answered the man meekly.

"In a bank?" demanded the banker, looking up brightly.

"No, sir; in a corn-store."

"Ah, I thought it couldn't have been in a bank. We are not so fortunate as to have men of your talents and enterprise in banks. But I interrupted you. Pray, proceed. You were about to say——" The invitation was accompanied by a gracious and encouraging wave of the left hand.

"I was thinking, sir, that it would be best if I went away of my own accord; and I thought I'd just mention this matter to you when I called with the guard ring of your good lady that's dead and gone."

"Quite right, quite right. And naturally you thought that I might be willing to lend you a hand on your way, partly out of feeling for you in your difficult position, and partly out of gratitude to you for your kind thoughtfulness in bringing me back the guard ring of poor Mrs. Grey."

The white forefinger of the white left hand went on quietly describing the circles, but the circles were one after the other increasing in circumference. The white right hand still rested on the edge of the partly-open drawer.

"That's it," said Farleg, with a sigh of relief. It was such a comfort to deal with a sensible man, a man who did most of the talking and thinking for you. "You know, sir, I found the rings——"

"Quite so, quite so."

Mr. Grey gave up describing circles, and for a while devoted himself to parallelograms. When he had finished each figure he regarded the invisible design for a while as though comparing the result of his labour with an ideal parallelogram. Then, becoming dissatisfied with his work, he began afresh.

" Quite so," he repeated, after a silence of a few moments. " You need not trouble yourself to go into detail. In fact, I prefer you should not, as my feelings are still much occupied with my great loss. Will you answer a few questions that may help to allay and soothe my feelings ? "

He ceased drawing the parallelograms, and looked up at the other with a glance of friendly enquiry.

Farleg threw himself back in his chair, and replied gravely : " I'll answer you, sir, any question it may please you to put."

" At what hour on the evening of the 17th did you break into this house ? "

" Eight o'clock."

" By Jove, Joe, you were an adventurous fellow to break into a house in daylight! I do think, in the face of such an enterprising spirit, you ought to seek a new country, where you would be properly appreciated. You have no chance here. Go to some place where the telegraph has not yet struck root. And yet for a man of your peculiar calling a dense population and civilisation are requisite. Your case, Joe, interests me a good deal, and, rely upon it, I shall always be glad to hear of your welfare and prosperity. I feel for you in your little difficulty, and I applaud your boldness. Fancy, breaking into a man's house at eight o'clock of an August evening! And how did you get in, Joe? I suppose by a ladder the workman had left against the wall?"

"Yes, sir. It was seeing a ladder against the wall that put the idea into my head."

The banker looked at Farleg with an expression of unlimited admiration.

"What a general you would make, Joe!" cried Mr. Grey, in pleasant enthusiasm. "You would use every bulrush as cover for your men! And so, when you saw the ladder against the wall, you thought to yourself you might as well slip up that ladder and have a look round? What a pushing man of business too! And you were alone?"

"Yes."

"You entered the tower first-floor, and gathered up a few things, this ring of my poor wife among the rest. But I don't think you went into any other room?"

"No, sir."

"And I don't think you could have been very long in the room; now, about how long?"

"Short of an hour. I heard you coming back, and I cleared out then."

"Ah! You heard me coming back,

and you cleared out then. Quite so. No doubt it was inconsiderate of me to come back and disturb you. But, you know, I was in a great state of anxiety and alarm — anxiety and alarm which were unfortunately only too well founded, as you, no doubt, have heard; we need not dwell on that painful event now. May I ask you if you have spoken of this affair to anyone?"

" No."

" Not to a soul?"

" Not to a soul."

" What a discreet general you would make! Upon my word I think you ought to go to California. San Francisco is the place for one so daring and so cautious. What a dashing cavalry leader you would make! And yet it would be a pity to throw you away on cavalry. Your natural place would be in the engineers."

Mr. Grey half closed his eyes, and gazed dreamily for a few seconds at the reclining figure of the man before him. Then hitching his chair a few inches nearer to the small table standing between him and Farleg, he said, in a drawling tone, as he softly slipped his hand into the drawer:

"I admire you for your ingenuity in availing yourself of that ladder, and for your boldness in entering the house in daylight. But I am completely carried away with enthusiasm when I think of your coming here to me, telling me this tale, and preserving the admirable calmness which you display. Indeed, Joe, I am amazed."

"Thank you, sir."

"Now, how much money did you think I'd be likely to give to help you out of this scrape, and out of this country?"

"Mr. Grey, you're a rich man."

The banker bowed and smiled.

"And that ring ought to be worth a heap of money to you."

"A guinea, or perhaps thirty shillings. At the very most I should say two pounds."

"But, sir, considering that it was your wife's, and that she wore it on the very day——"

"Quite so. On the very day of her wedding——"

"That is not what I meant——"

"But that is the aspect of the affair which endears the ring to me. Pray let us keep to the business in hand. You bring me a ring which I own I should not like you to have kept from me. You make me a present of this ring, and you ask me to help you out of the country. Now, how much would be sufficient to help you out of the country, and settle you and your wife comfortably in a new home ? "

" A thousand pounds."

" A thousand pounds ! My dear Joe, if you were about to represent the majesty of the kingdoms of Great Britain and Ireland at a foreign court, you could ask little more for travelling-expenses and commencing existence. A thousand pounds ! What a lucrative business yours must have been to make you hope you could get a thousand pounds for the goodwill of it ! "

" But it is not every day a thing like this turns up. You have a lot of waiting before you get your chance. In fact, my chance did not belong to the ordinary business at all."

" Quite so. It was a kind of perquisite. Well, now, Joe, don't you think if I gave you twenty-five pounds as a present it would fully provide for your outward voyage?" Mr. Grey made the proposal with a winning and an enticing gesture of his left hand.

Farleg looked down at his boots again, and said very slowly, and with an accent that left no doubt of his earnestness and determination :

"It isn't often a chance of this kind turns up, and I can't afford to let it pass ; no honest man could afford to let it pass, and I have a wife looking to me. You have no one looking to you, not even a wife—not even a wife."

"Quite so."

"Well, I want the money. I want to try and get an honest start in life, and I think I shall buy land——"

"Out of the thousand pounds?" queried Mr. Grey, with a look of amused enjoyment.

"Out of the thousand pounds you are going to give me. Can't you see," added

Farleg, sitting up in his chair, leaning both his elbows on the small table between them, " can't you see it's to your advantage as well as mine to give me a large sum ? "

"Candidly I cannot," answered Mr. Grey, tapping Farleg encouragingly on the shoulder with his white left hand. "Tell me how it is. I am quite willing to be convinced."

" Well, if I take your five-and-twenty, I spend it here, or I spend it getting there, and then I'm stranded, don't you see, sir ? "

"Go on." With two soft appreciative pats from the left white hand.

"Of course, as soon as I find myself hard up I come to you, or I write to you for more, and that would only be wasting your time."

" But," said Mr. Grey, with a sly look and a sly wag of his head, "if you got

the thousand you might spend it here
or there, and then you might again be
applying to me. Ah, no! Joe, I don't
think it would do to give you that thousand. You can have the twenty-five now,
if you like."

" Well, sir, I've looked into the matter
deeper than that. When you give me
the thousand, I and my wife will leave
this country, go to America, out West,
and buy land. There we shall settle
down as respectable people, and it would
be no advantage to me to rake up the
past, once I was settled down and prosperous. So, sir, if you please, I'll have
the thousand."

There was respectful resolution in
Farleg's voice as he spoke. The faces of
the two men were not more than a foot
apart now. They were looking as straight
into one another's eyes as two experienced
fencers when the play begins. Mr. Grey's

face ceased to move, and took a settled
expression of gracious badinage.

"I think, Joe," said he, "that I can
manage the matter more economically than
your way."

"What is that way, sir?"

"As I told you before, I look on you
as a very enterprising man. First, you
break into a man's house in daylight, and
then you come and beard the lion in his
den. You come to the man whose house
you honoured by a visit through a window,
and you say to him—I admit that nothing
could have been in better taste than your
manner of saying it——"

"Thank you, sir, but you took me so
kindly and so gentleman-like."

"Thank *you*, Joe; but I mustn't com-
pliment you again, or 'we shall get no
farther than compliments to-night. As I
was saying, you ask him for no less than
a thousand pounds to help you out of

the country and into a respectable line of life. Indeed, all my sympathy is with you in your good intention, but then I have to think of myself——"

"But you're a rich man, sir, and to you a thousand pounds isn't much, and it's everything to me. It will make me safe, and help me out of a way of life I never took to until driven to it," pleaded Farleg. .

"Well put, very well put. Now, this is my position. This is my plan; let me hear what you think of it: On the night or evening of the 17th you break into my house; on the night or evening of the 27th you visit me for some purpose or other——"

"To give you back your dead wife's ring."

"Quite so. You may be sure I am overlooking no point in the case. Let me proceed with my view. You and I don't

get on well together, and you attack me.
You are clearly the burglar, and I am
attacked by you, and I defend myself with
force.   You kill me ; that is no good to
you.   You won't make a penny by my
death.   But suppose it should unhappily
occur that the revolver, on the trigger of
which, Joe, I now have my finger, and
the muzzle of which is about a foot from
your heart, suppose it should go off, what
then ? You can see the accident would
be all in my favour."

Farleg uttered a loud whistle.

For a second no word was spoken.   No
movement was made in that room.

All at once, apparently from the feet
of the two men, a wild alarmed scream of
a woman shot up through the silence, and
shook the silence into echoes of chattering
fear.

As though a blast had struck the
banker's face, it shrivelled up like a

withered leaf. Something heavy fell from his hand in the drawer, and he rose slowly, painfully, to his feet.

Farleg rose also, keeping his face in the same relation, and on the same level as the banker's, until the pinched face of the banker stole slowly above the burglar's.

The hands of Grey rested on the table. His eyes were fixed on vacancy. He seemed to be listening intently, spellbound by some awful vision, some distracting anticipation intimately concerned with appalling voices.

Slowly from his lips trickled the whispered words : " What was that ? "

" *My* wife's voice," whispered Farleg. "You thought it was *yours*. When I told you no one knew, I meant I had no pal. But my wife knows *all*, and if anything came amiss to me she'd tell all."

" I understand," the banker answered, still in a whisper. The dread was slowly descending from his face, and he made a hideous attempt at a smile.

" I, too," pursued Farleg, " was afraid we might quarrel, and left her there. For one whistle she was to scream out to show she was on the watch. For two whistles she was to run away and call help. Do you see, sir ? "

" Very clever. Very neat. You have won the odd trick."

" And honours are divided."

" Yes. How is that money to reach you ? "

" I'd like it in gold, sir, if you please. You can send it in a large parcel, a hamper, sir, or a large box, so that no one need be the wiser. I'm for your own good as well as my own in this matter."

" You shall have the money the day after to-morrow at four o'clock. It will reach you from London. Now go."

" Well, after what has been done, and our coming to a bargain, shake hands, Wat," said the man, in a tone of insolent triumph.

" Go, sir. Go at once!"

" Honours are not divided ; I hold three to your one. Give me your hand, old man. Joe Farleg will never split on a pal."

With a shudder of loathing the banker held out his hand.

As soon as he was alone, the moment the door was shut, he took up the claret-jug, poured the contents over his right hand to cleanse it from the contamination of that touch, and then walked hastily up and down the room, waving his hand through the air until it dried.

" A thousand isn't much to secure him. But will it secure him ? That is the question. Yes, I think it will. I think the coast is now clear. With prudence

and patience I can do all now," he
whispered to himself, with his left hand
on his forehead. "Wat Grey, you've
had a close shave. Nothing could have
been closer. Had you pulled that trigger
all would have been lost. Now you have
a clear stage, and must let things take
their course. The old man can't live for
ever; and until he dies you must keep
quiet and repress all indication of the
direction in which your hopes lie. Maud
does not dream of this."

A knock at the door.

"Come in."

James, the servant, entered, holding
a slip of paper in his hand.

"What is it, James?" asked the
master.

"That man that's gone out, sir, said
he forgot to give his address, and as you
might want it he asked me to take it up
to you."

Mr. Grey was standing by the low gasalier as the servant handed him the piece of paper.

Mr. Grey took the address in his right hand; as he did so the purblind footman sprang back a pace.

"What's the matter?" demanded Mr. Grey with an amused smile.

"Ex—excuse — me — sir," the man faltered, "but your hand——"

"Well, what about it?"

"It's all over blood!"

"What! What do you say?" shouted the master, in a tone of dismay. "Do *you* want a thousand too?"

"Indeed, no, sir; and I beg pardon; but do look at your hand."

Mr. Grey held up his hand, examined it, and then burst out into a loud shout of laughter. When he could speak he cried:

"You charming idiot! You will kill

me with your droll ways. That dirty
wretch who went out touched my hand.
I had no water near me, so I poured
some claret over my hand and forgot to
wipe it."

He approached James and held out
his hand, saying, "Look." Then added,
in a tone of solemn amusement: "James,
there was once a man who died of laughing
at seeing an ass eat. I do think I shall
die of laughing at hearing a donkey talk.
Bring me the coffee. Go."

And as the servant was leaving the
room, Mr. Grey broke out into a laugh
of quiet self-congratulation on the fact of
his possessing such a wonderful source of
amusement in his servant, James.

CHAPTER III.

THE MANOR HOUSE.

THE house occupied by Mr. Grey was
very old. It had been the Manor House,
and was still called the Manor House, or
the Manor, although it had long ago
ceased to be the property of the original
owner's descendants. For years before
Mr. Grey bought it the house had been
uninhabited.

It bore a bad name—why, no one
could tell. The fortunes of the lords
of the manor had gradually mouldered
away, and the old house had been allowed
to fall into decay and dilapidation.

During the time it was shut up

people spoke of it as a kind of phantom house; some regarded it as a myth, and others treated it with a superstitious respect as a thing which might exercise an evil influence over those who fell under the shadow of its displeasure.

Sunken deeply from the road, surrounded by a wild tangle of rugged oaks, its grounds girt with walls ten feet high, there were few points open to the public from which a glimpse of it could be caught, and no spot from which a full view could be obtained.

Boys had scaled the walls and penetrated into the tangled mazes of the neglected undergrowth. But the briars and brambles and bushes were too rough even for boys, and they came away soon.

No boy of Daneford—and there were high - hearted, brave, adventurous boys there — could say he had penetrated

as far as the house. Although those who
had once been boys of Daneford had
faced the enemies of their country in
every clime, by day and by night, on
land and sea, and although the boys of
that city, at the time spoken of, were
made of as stout stuff and inspired by
as gallant hearts as the boys who had
fought and fallen in Spain, India, America,
Belgium, Egypt, where you will, not one
of all of them would dare, alone and by
night, to break through that jungle, and
penetrate to that house.

The soil of the Manor Park was
low and full of rich juices, and fertile
with long rest, so the vegetation beneath
the gnarled boughs of the interlacing oaks
could hold the moisture well when the
sun was hot, and from that ground to
the sun they never saw clearly rose huge
green and red and yellow slimy weeds
among the brambles and the shrubs.

From the nests of many generations
of birds which had built in those distorted
trees seeds of all things that grow on
this land had fallen, and taken root
and prospered in the rich ground of
the sultry glens and caverns formed by
the scraggy arms and foliage of the oaks;
year after year this disorderly growth
had burst up out of the fat, greasy soil
in unwholesome profusion, unclean luxury,
and had rotted down again into the over-
lush earth. So that the spring-root and
ground-fruit, and all manner of green
things, jostled and crushed one another,
and the weaker were strangled and eaten
up by the stronger.

Thousands of birds yearly built in the
trees of the Manor Park; for here came
no guns to kill or scare, no boys to pilfer
the eggs or young ones; and this republic
of birds over-head was a source of great
profit to the soil below.

Often birds fell from the trees dead of cold in the winter nights, and when the sun shone out the industrious mole came and buried them decently, and their bones were of service to the soil.

The mole, too, was useful in another way, for he turned up the clay now and then, here and there, and opened avenues into the earth for water burdened with fructifying juices.

And here, too, was that ever-active sexton of the vegetable world, the fungus. In the vast winds of the winters, when the oaks gored one another, and tore off the fangs of their antlers, great boughs fell with shrieks to the earth. Later the sexton fungus crept over to the shattered limbs and lodged on them, and ate them up silently and slowly, and then the fungus itself melted into the earth.

Here were worms of enormous growth, and frogs and toads, and snails and

lizards, and all other kinds of slimy
insects and reptiles, and the boys said
snakes, but snakes were put forward in
excuse of fear on the part of the boys.
There were no hares, no rabbits, no deer,
no cows, no sheep, no goats, nor any of
the gentle creatures that put grass and
green things to uses profitable to man.

Here in those vaults of sickly twilight
vegetable nature held high saturnalia, un-
disturbed save by the seasons and worms
and snails and caterpillars and slugs. This
was not a prosperous field, a prudent grove,
a stately wood, a discreet garden; it was
a robber's cave of the green world, in
which the plunder of all the fields lay
heaped without design, for no good or
useful end.

At night the darkness was thick and
hot in these blind alleys and inexplorable
aisles. When the foot was put down something slipped beneath it, a greasy branch,

a viscous fruit, a reptile, or the fat stalk of some large-leafed ground-plant.

The trunks of the trees and the branches of the shrubs were damp with gelatinous dews. If there was a moon, something might always be seen sliding silently through the grass or leaves and pulpy roots.

Strange and depressing odours of decay came stealthily upon the sense now and then, and filled the mind with hints of unutterable fears. If in the branches above a sleeping bird chirped or fluttered, it seemed as though the last bird left was stealing away from the fearful place. The fat reptiles that glided and slipped in the ghostly moonlight were fleeing, and leaving you alone to behold some spectacle, encounter some fate, too repulsive for the contemplation of reason.

Within this belt of rank vegetation and oaks the Manor House stood. The house had a plain stone front with small narrow windows, three on each side of the main door. At the rear was a large paved court-yard, with a pump and horse-trough in the middle.

The chief building consisted of a ground-floor, on which were the reception-rooms; a first floor of bedrooms; and a second floor; the windows of which were dormar, intended for the servants of the establishment.

The walls of the house were of great thickness and strength. On the ground and first floors most of the doorways into the passages had double doors. Owing to the great thickness of the walls, and the double doors, and the massive floorings and partition walls, sounds, even the loudest, travelled with great difficulty through that house.

In front of the house stretched a broad gravelled drive, which narrowed into a gravelled road as it set off to the main

road, a considerable distance farther on.
This carriage - road wound in and out
through the oaks of the Park. Between
the gravelled open in front of the house
and the trees stretched a narrow band
of shaven grass. This narrow band of
grass followed the carriage-road up to the
lodge-gate.

Around the paved yard in the rear
stood the coach-house, stables, kitchen,
laundry, scullery, larder, and other offices,
and still farther to the rear of the house,
behind the yard, were the flower and
kitchen gardens. To the rear of all,
surrounding all, and binding all in like
suffocating bondage, was the Park of
gnarled oaks and rank lush undergrowth
and slimy soil.

In looking at the house you were
not conscious of anything uncanny or
repulsive. At the left-hand end—that is,
the end of the house nearest to Daneford

—there rose a tower, mounting only one storey above the dormar floor.

Upon the top of this tower was a huge iron tank, corroded into a skeleton of its former self. Looking at that weather-battered and rusted tank, with the under-growth in the Park behind you, the former resembled the decay of the indomitable natives of America, who perished slowly in opposing themselves to fate; the over-ripe prosperity of the latter looked like the destruction of the Romans, who ate and drank and slept their simplicity and their manhood away.

One peculiarity of this house was that no green plant or creeper could get a living out of its dry walls. Neither on the house nor on the tower had ever been seen one leaf native to the place. Here was another thing in strong contrast to the teeming vegetation environing this house.

It was not while looking at the Manor
you felt its unpleasant influence. In
sunshine nothing disturbed your peace
while you contemplated its dry, cold front.
But when you had gone away; when you
were sitting in your own bright room;
when you were walking along a lonely
road; when you awoke in the middle
of the night, and heard the torrents
of the storm roar as they whirled round
your window; then, if the thought of that
house came up before your mind, you
shrank back from its image as from an
apparition of evil mission. In your mental
vision the house itself seemed scared and
afeared.

The intense green life that dwelt
beneath those oaks stood out in startling
contrast with the absolute nudity of those
unapparelled stones. The house seemed to
shrink instinctively from any contact with
verdure, as though it felt assured of evil

from moss or leaf or blade. It appeared to dread that the oaks would creep up on it and overwhelm it in their portentous shadows, beat it down with their giant arms.

That tower stood out in the imagination like an arm uplifted in appeal; that shattered tank became a tattered flag of distress. The windows looked like scared eyes, the broad doorway a mouth gaping with terror. The whole building quivered with human horror, was silent with frozen awe.

In the year 1856 Henry Walter Grey's father died, and the son became sole proprietor of the Daneford Bank. Up to that time the son had lived, with his wife, to whom he had then been married six years, in the Bank-house as manager under his father. There were only a few years' lease of his father's suburban residence to run, and a likelihood arose that the landlord would not renew, so young Grey had to look out for a home, as he intended appointing a manager and living away from the office.

At that time the Manor House was in the market, and Mr. Grey bought it for, as he said, "a song, and a very poor song, too," considering the extent of the Park, the value of the timber, and the spacious old house. As a matter of fact, no one valued the dwelling at a penny beyond what the sale of its stones would bring; for the impression of the seller was that, owing to its uncanny aspect and bad name, no one would think of buying it to live in.

All Daneford was taken by surprise when it heard that young Grey, Wat Grey, Wat had bought the fearful Manor House in which no family had lived for generations, and from which even the furniture and servants had been long since withdrawn. Did he mean to take it down, build a new house, and effect a wholesome clearance of those odious groves?

No, he had answered, with a light laugh, he harboured no intention of knocking down the old house to please the neighbours; of course he was going to repair the house, and when it was fully restored he would ask his friends to come and try if beef and mutton tasted worse, or wine was less cheering, under that roof because nervous people had been pleased to frighten themselves into fits over the Park and the Manor House.

In a year the house had been put into thorough order, and even the tower had not been wholly neglected, for one room of it, that on a level with Mr. Grey's own bedroom, had been completely renovated into a kind of extra dressing-room to Mr. Grey's bed-

room, from which a short passage led
to it.

Nothing was done to the ground-
floor of the tower; nothing was done to
the floor on a level with the dormar ;
nothing was done with the floor above
the dormar.

Nothing was done to the unsightly
tank on the top of the tower.

With respect to the rooms of the
tower, Mr. Grey said he had no need of
more than the one.

With respect to the tank, he said he
would in no way try to diminish the
unprepossessing aspect of the exterior of
the house ; he would rely upon the
interior, the good cheer and the welcome
beneath the roof, to countervail the ill-
omened outer walls.

There was another reason, too, Mr.
Grey said, why he had made up his mind
to alter nothing in the surrounding grounds

or outward aspect of the house—he wanted to see whether that house was going to beat him, or he was going to beat that house.

So when all was in order, he set about house-warming on a prodigious scale—a scale that was a revelation to the people of Daneford.

He filled all the bedrooms with guests, and had a couple of dozen men to dine with him every day for a fortnight.

He told his servants, as long as they did their work punctually and satisfactorily, they might have friends to see them, and might make their friends welcome to the best things in the servants' hall every day for a fortnight.

There were bonfires in the courtyard, and fiddlers and dancing. A barrel of beer was placed on the horse-trough, and mugs and cans appeared in glittering rows on a table beside the cask, and painted on the butt-end of the cask the words, "Help yourself."

When he lived in town his establishment had consisted of three servants. For the fête a dozen additional servants were engaged and a French cook. There were a lodge and gate to the Manor Park, but there was no lodge-man or woman; and during the festivities the gate always stood open until midnight, and all passers-by were free to come in and join the dancers and partake of the ale.

One day he had all the clerks of his own bank to dine with him; and while they were over their wine and cigars he informed them their salaries were from that hour advanced twenty per cent.

He was then a simple member of the Chamber of Commerce; he had not yet been elected chairman. He entertained the whole Chamber another evening, and then told the members he had that day written to their secretary, declaring his resolution not to charge interest on the money advanced by his bank — three thousand pounds—for the completion of the new building in course of construction by the Chamber.

A third evening he asked all the members of the Harbour Board, and told them that he had made up his mind to abandon the old claim for interest on their overdraughts set up by his father.

Then he gave a Commercial Club evening, to which were bidden all his friends and acquaintances, who were also members of the club. After roast beef came two large silver dishes, on one of which was, plainly enough, plum-pudding ; on the other, something that was plainly not plum-pudding. The host nodded to the servants, and both dishes burst into flame ; the dish that contained the plum-pudding standing opposite the treasurer of the club, at the foot of the table; the thing that was not plum-pudding standing opposite the banker. Whatever had been before him was, when the brandy ceased to burn, all consumed, except a little black matter that floated about on the surface of the fluid in the dish.

"Everyone must have some of my new sauce. I invented it myself, and I will take it as a favour if all will ·taste it with the pudding."

All partook of it and praised it highly, and many said they had never tasted its like before, and several began elaborate analyses of it, and minute comparisons between it and a hundred of well-known sauces.

After a while he said: "The roast beef and plum-pudding of Old England for ever!" Then pointing to the dish containing the floating black matter before him, "And the ashes of my mortgage on the club property once!"

The Boat Club were his guests another evening, and a large gold loving-cup was brought in and carried about with a rich compound of dark wines and stimulating spices, and out of this all were to drink. When all had tasted and toasted in the common cup the object of their common solicitude, the last man after drinking called out that there was something which rattled and jingled and slid about in the bottom of the cup. The master of the house seemed more inquisitive than any of the others, bade the finder spill out the contents of the cup on a salver, and, behold, one hundred and five new sovereigns fresh from the Mint! Upon this discovery the host rose and said that love was the rarest of alchemy, and that the touch of a score of loyal lips, all having the one interest at heart, had changed the liquor into gold for the good of the club, and that the gold and the cup must go together to the club.

When he had the organisers and directors of the Poor's Christmas Coal Fund to dinner, each member found, folded up in his napkin, twenty orders, each order for five shillings' worth of coal.

Such generous and kindly deeds, and such cordial hospitality, could not but endear him to the people of Daneford; and by reason of his knowing so many men intimately, and each one of these men being more or less proud of the acquaintance, they all called him "Wat," to show how very intimate they were with him, and to show that in the best commercial set in Daneford there was no one else known by the name of Wat. They called him Wat in preference to Henry or Harry, because there is not perhaps among all the Christian names one which admits of such an intimately familiar contraction as Walter.

But all the banqueting and largess did not disenchant the ominous mansion.

Those who had been at the prodigal house-warming always remembered the exterior aspect of the house when the revels were at their height as even worse than the ordinary appearance; for the small red windows in the thick dark walls looked at night like the eyes of a desperate man who had drank deeply to keep up his courage in some supreme ordeal. And by day ever afterwards, to those who had been in the house at the festival, it seemed as though the house looked more aghast than ever, like the face of one who, having slept off the artificial courage, had awaked to reduced resources and increased dangers.

CHAPTER IV.

AN UNSELFISH MOTHER.

ALL the parties given by Mr. Grey at
the Manor House were men's parties. Mrs.
Grey rarely or never was to be found
in the drawing-room after dinner; and,
indeed, the drawing-room was seldom
lighted up.

Mrs. Grey was a pretty, low-sized, dark-
eyed, nervous woman, a few years the
junior of her husband. He had met her
first in London, in a house where she
was staying on a visit with friends. She
was alone in the world, had a small
fortune, which, while it made her no

object of pursuit in the circle she frequented, kept her independent.

There was a little mystery and a little doubt about her, and while neither the mystery nor the doubt was sufficient to disquiet anyone, it served to keep interest in her alive, and the more prudent and calculating of suitors from love-making. Individually she was popular; but while those who knew her spoke well of her in her absence, the good things said of her always began in superlatives, and, as the conversation went on, diminished to positives, and the talk usually ended with a vague "but" and an unfinished sentence.

Perhaps she was a little odd, they said. Perhaps she had French blood in her veins. Perhaps the strange blood was Spanish. She had a look not wholly English—a look denoting no close kinship with any other people. Her name was

Muir, which seemed to indicate that she
came of a stock north of the Tweed. Yet
she had never been in Scotland, nor her
father before her, nor anyone of his
side, as far as he could trace back. Her
mother had been the daughter of a Truro
solicitor, her father a member of the
Equity bar of London. Those who had
known her father and mother declared
that she resembled neither in her face
nor her manner. She was dark, low-
sized, and odd; they had both been
tall, fair, and models of conventional
insipidity.

When Henry Walter Grey married
Miss Muir she was twenty-four years of
age, he twenty-nine. The women judged
her to be thirty-four, the men allowed
that she might be twenty-seven; but all
agreed that young Grey, with his prospects,
might have done much better as far as
money went.

But among the young and the chivalric
of Daneford, young Grey helped forward
his nascent popularity by marrying a poor
wife and risking his father's displeasure
for his sweetheart's sake. The young and
chivalric of Daneford were never tired of
pointing to the pleasantest and most prosperous man in the city as one who had
made his love paramount above all other
considerations in the selection of a wife.

From the time he won his wife until
he lost her his manner towards her gained
him daily increase of respect among the
people of the city. Every indulgence and
luxury which his position could afford were
lavished upon her. Wives who had cause
of displeasure or dissatisfaction with their
husbands always cited Mr. Grey as a
shining contrast to their own too economical
or exacting lords. It was not alone that
she was never denied anything for which
she could reasonably care, but, notwith-

standing the clubs and the institutions and the boards of which Mr. Grey was a member, no more domestic man lived in Dancford. He always dined at home, except on occasions of great public interest; and when he had no guests he sat reading or conversing with her, or they both went for a stroll in the fine twilight, or visited the theatre, or any other form of public amusement afforded by the town.

· As the years of their married life glided by, and no child came to make an endearing interruption to the smooth course of wedded sweethearts, the attachment between the husband and wife seemed to borrow a greater depth from the soft melancholy arising out of their childless condition. It was, the town said, a thousand pities the rich, amiable, amusing, good-looking Wat Grey had no one to leave his fine business and his vast fortune to.

If a friend alluded to the fact of his

childlessness he always put the subject
aside with as little humour and as much
gentleness as the character of the speaker
allowed of. To his wife, who often made
tearful allusions to the circumstance, he
replied with cheerful hopefulness, and bade
her set her grief for him away, as he was
quite content and happy with the bles-
sings Heaven had already sent him, chief
among which was a wife he loved.

Although Mrs. Grey did not go into
society, and had no ladies to dinner, she
had a few visiting friends upon whom
she called in turn, and who learned from
her the uniform kindliness of her husband,
and the great gentleness with which he
accepted the absence of an heir or heiress.

In fact, the more people heard of
Mr. Grey, the more he grew in popular
esteem, and behind all this amiability on
his part there was a factor which hugely
multiplied its value. At first, when he

brought his wife home to Daneford, and the people of his set began to know her a little, they all declared that she was pretty, very pretty, and a trifle odd.

Time went on, and although she lost none of her prettiness with her years—hers being the beauty that depends on bone and outline, and not on surface and colour—her peculiarities gained upon her; and whether, the Daneford folk said, it was the foreign blood that darkened her eyes and her hair and her ways, or a slight strain of madness, they could not decide, but she was, beyond all doubt, not in manner like the average English-woman of her class.

At first her peculiarities defied defini-tion. People said she was very nice, but a little queer, cracked, crazy. She was very impulsive, and sometimes incoherent. No action of hers seemed the result of forethought or preparation. She ordered

the servants to bring this, that, or the
other thing, and when they came with it
she told them they might take it away
again, as she had changed her mind. She
ordered the brougham for four, went
out walking at a quarter to four, and
stayed out till six, without countermanding
the brougham.

About the time that Mr. Grey bought
the Manor House, Mrs. Grey had a difference with her cook, and her cook left her
in a violent temper. The cook had been
with her ever since Mrs. Grey had first
come to Daneford, and was the confidential
servant of her mistress. Soon after the
cook had left it reached the ears of a few
acquaintances of Mr. Grey that a dreadful
spectre had appeared in his household.
The fact that Mrs. Grey had now
been married some years and was still
childless had preyed very deeply on her
excitable temperament, and, dreadful to

say, she not unfrequently took more wine
than was good for her.

Those who heard this now saw a reason,
unguessed by others, why the banker
bought that odious house swathed round
with that fearful wood. There his wife
would be secluded, free from prying eyes
and guarded against any close daily contact
with neighbours. How had it been kept
secret so long? The cook, now discharged,
had obtained for the unhappy woman
what she wanted, and the poor lady was
wonderfully discreet and · cautious, and
until that servant went no one but
the cook and the afflicted husband
ever dreamed of such a thing. It was
dreadful.

But the most intimate friend of Grey
never knew from him, by even the faintest
hint, there was a single cloud over his
domestic happiness.

He always spoke of his wife in terms

of the most tender consideration and kindliness. He was by no means weak or
uxorious; but there was a loyal trust, an
ever-active sympathy in him towards her,
that won greatly on the young and old
men and women of Daneford.

The evil circumstance under which
Mrs. Grey laboured was never an open
scandal in the town. In the first place,
owing to her own great prudence and
circumspection, no one had any suspicion
of the melancholy fact from herself. If
she was the victim of a debasing weakness,
she never betrayed herself publicly, and
those who heard of it through indirect
ways had kept the secret closely, out of
respect to the man whose fame and name
and popularity stood so high among his
fellow-citizens. Indeed, some who heard
the rumour disbelieved it wholly, and
declared their conviction that it was the
malicious invention of a discharged servant,

based on the eccentric habits and unfamiliar ways of the poor lady.

But the fact remained that, even to the spacious Manor House, no lady guests were invited to dinner; no lady guests stayed for twenty-four hours; and, beyond a few afternoon callers, no ladies visited the house at all. But perhaps in Daneford there were not a dozen families in possession of the fact that would account for the strict retirement in which the mistress of the Manor lived, and the young and the chivalric continued to look on Grey and his wife as not only the most prosperous, but also the most happy, couple in the whole county.

Very soon after Henry Grey's marriage with Miss Muir, he found out that she did not possess the solid good sense and grave discernment essential in the confidant of a banker.

She not only lacked the golden faculty

of silence, but dealt with facts communicated to her in a most imaginative and injudicious manner. He told her that a substantial and solvent merchant of the town had overdrawn his account five hundred pounds. Shortly after, the merchant's wife called on Mrs. Grey, and the latter, in a moment of communicativeness, said to the former that business was in a bad way, and that she understood the former's husband owed the Bank, over and above ordinary business, no less a sum than five thousand pounds. The merchant's wife related this to her husband, and he came in great indignation to Grey. Mr. Grey said his wife's talk had been only woman's gossip, and that he had most certainly never told his wife or any one else the merchant owed the Bank five thousand pounds over-draught.

The merchant said he was quite sure Mr. Grey had not, but urged that something of the over-draught must have been communicated to Mrs. Grey, and that a woman's gossip was quite capable of ruining a solvent man.

On another occasion the banker told her the Bank had not made as much money that year as the year before, and she informed some chance callers that the Bank was losing heavily. This rumour might have shaken the credit of an institution less solidly established than the Daneford Bank; but in the city and country surrounding the city the Bank was looked upon as much more safe than the Bank of England, insomuch as the Threadneedle Street concern had a paper currency, and the Daneford did not mortgage any of its capital by such an issue, and stood in no temptation to diminish its stock of gold or overstep safety.

These two experiences of Grey's, coupled with a few others of less importance but

similar nature, convinced him that the
more general and abstract his statements
of business matters to his wife the better,
and from the moment he arrived at this
conclusion he carried it into effect. She,
having no talent for the particular, did
not seem to miss his confidence, and
remained perfectly content with common-
place generalities as to business matters.
Indeed, having very little of the highly
feminine virtue of inquisitiveness, she was
not much interested in business statements
of any kind.

Most men will talk more freely to a
woman whom they trust than to any man,
no matter how near to them by ties of
nature or affection. Henry Grey was no
exception to the rule, and when he found
he durst no longer confide important
secrets to his wife, he unburdened himself
to another woman, a widow, now past
seventy, but still straight and intelligent,

and sympathetic and hale, a woman who
had won and retained a most powerful
hold upon his esteem, affection, and confidence—his mother.

Whilst all the world of Daneford was
calculating the enormous fortune the Dane-.
ford Bank must be making for its owner,
and was bemoaning the fact that Wat
Grey had no child to leave his fine business
and his vast savings to, there were two
people the nature of whose anxiety about
Mr. Grey's affairs did not take the same
course.

These two people were the only beings
possessing knowledge of the condition
of Mr. Grey's private fortune and the
bank.

For years he had kept the true state
of affairs from his mother, but at length,
as blow succeeded blow, he could no longer
bear the burden of his secret, and he un-
folded it to her. He did not trouble her

with detail, but informed her briefly that he had backed the South in the American wars—that not only had he lost all his own private fortune, but of the depositors' money as well.

At first she was overwhelmed with surprise and horror to think the splendid business and reputation made for the Bank by her dead husband and his father before him should be ruined by her son, and that not only had the Bank been ruined and her son's fortune and position destroyed, but the moneys of the clients had also been included in the horrible disaster.

But, despite her seventy years, she was a brave old lady, full of honour and spirits and courage. Once the first shock was over, she set all her faculties at work to try and sustain the drooping energies of her only son.

She know he was not free from troubles

at home; she knew he gave none of his business confidences to his wife. Though she deplored these facts, she felt there was no help for them; and if at first reluctant to assist him in councils which ought to be held between him and his wife, in the end she saw it would be the wisest course for her to listen, to encourage him to speak, and to aid him with any advice she might think it wise to give.

Apparently, however, the affairs of the Bank were beyond the aid of advice. At every interview between mother and son he assured her he saw no opening in the clouds; that, in fact, they got blacker and blacker as time wore on.

Towards the beginning of 1866 things had, the son told the mother, come to the worst.

"All is lost," he said; "all is lost. I have been staving off and staving off until everything has got into a hopeless

tangle, out of which I can find but one
thing—ruin !"

"Then, Henry, I suppose you must
shut the door; and as you see nothing
else for it, the sooner you stop up the
better."

"Mother, the day I shut the Bank
door I'll open another door."

"What do you mean ?"

"I'll open the door into the other
world with a charge of gunpowder."

"Don't say such a foolish, dreadful
thing! You are not, I hope, such a
coward as to fly from the consequences
of your own act. If you have lost the
money in fair trading you need not be
ashamed to meet them all; others beside
you lost by that unfortunate South. Your
father would have stood his ground and
faced the city," said the old woman, with
spirit and pride.

"No doubt, mother, no doubt my

father would have had the manliness to
stand and face the break; but he was a
man of great endurance and nerve; you
know I am not. I would do anything
rather than meet such a crash and live
after it. You know I have been much
more out in the world than my father.
I am mixed up with such a number of
things, am closely connected with such a
number of institutions and men, that
nothing, no consideration, could induce me
to outlive bankruptcy. The people would
not believe facts; they would not credit
any statement, however plain, that I was
insolvent. They would say that I had
appropriated the money of the depositors,
made a fraudulent pretence of bankruptcy,
and concealed the money for my own use.
I know the world better than you, mother;
I know the world, and what it would say.
I may be popular now; but if I fell, the
street-boys might kick me through the

gutter and no one would take my part, or try to get me fair play."

He dropped his head into his hands and shuddered.

The old woman looked at him with a sad sympathy, which was not wholly destitute of reproach.

"You know, Henry, thousands of men have had to face such things, and have come out of their difficulties without a stain or a hard word——"

"In my case that is impossible. I tell you, mother, they would have no more mercy on me than on a snake. The Bank is a private one, the property of one person, and on that one person all the wrath would fall. It is not like a joint stock, or a limited liability, where many are concerned as principals or shareholders or directors. It would be a case between an individual and his creditors. It would look as if I had borrowed money privately of all the people I knew, and spent it or gambled in dangerous foreign speculations, until I had dissipated their last pennies and left the people beggars. No, mother; the day I shut the Bank door I open the gate of Eternity with a bullet."

He was walking up and down his mother's drawing-room, with his hands clasped behind ·his coat, his eyes bent on the ground, and a look of concentrated thought upon his usually placid and beaming features.

" I will not hear you say that again, Henry," cried the mother, stamping her foot impatiently on the floor. "Listen to me. You know my two thousand a year is clear of the Bank——"

" Thank Heaven and my father for that ! " cried Grey earnestly.

" Can't you shut up the Bank, and you and Bee "—Beatrice, his wife—" come and stay with me for a while ? We could

leave England and live on a thousand a
year in the south of France, or anywhere
you like, and save up a thousand a year
to start you again——"

"I would die ten thousand deaths, dear
mother, rather than touch your money,"
he cried fervently, catching her hand and
holding it in both his, and opening his
hands now and then to kiss the shrivelled
hand which had once, when soft and full,
joined his — then softer and fuller — in
prayer, and now, when he was strong and
she was weak, tried to shield and succour
him as in the days when he was a little
child.

"Don't be sentimental at such a crisis,"
cried his mother petulantly. "You shall
do as I say; or if you like, when the Bank
affair is settled, we can sell the annuity.
I know I'm old, and it's not worth many
years' purchase; but we should get a few
thousand for it, and that would give you

a fresh start in some other business. Now I tell you this is what *shall* happen. Do you hear me? I will not wait for your consent; this very day I will see about selling the annuity—what do you call it? capitalising it? Go, Henry, and no more nonsense about gunpowder and bullets. Such things are only fit for the stage or the Continent, and are quite beneath the notice of a sensible English man of business."

He rose to his feet and cried: "You shall not, you must not, mother. I have been making out things worse than they really are. I am depressed and ill. Believe me, there is no need for doing what you say. There is one venture of mine, in no way connected with the late war, the greatest of all my ventures; and although I do not look on it as a very safe or sound venture, it may come all right yet. I shall know in a fortnight. You must promise me to do nothing until then. Promise me, my dear mother!"

He spoke eagerly, passionately; and as he uttered the final words he caught both her hands in his, and looked beseechingly into her eyes.

"And in a fortnight you will tell me?" she asked, looking searchingly into his face.

"In a fortnight I will tell you."

"And between this and then you will not, in my presence or in your own secret mind, speak or think about such nonsense as daggers or poison-bowls, or gunpowder or bullets?" she asked scornfully.

"I promise I will not."

"Very well," she said; "I will do nothing till I hear from you at the end of a fortnight. Let us shake hands, Henry, and part friends."

"Friends!" he exclaimed, as tears of love and sorrow came into his eyes.

"Mother, you are the only one on earth I love now."

"Hush, sir! How dare you say such a thing!"

"I swear it!" he cried vehemently. "I would do anything, dare anything, for you, mother——"

"And for your wife," she added, as if reminding him of an omission made in carelessness.

He paid no attention to her suggestion.

"You are the only one in the world who knows me really."

"And longest," she added, with a bright smile. "There—go now, Henry; this scene is growing theatrical or Continental, and unbecoming the drawing-room of an English mother. There—go."

And she hustled him to the door, opened the door, thrust him out, and closed the door upon him.

As soon as she was sure he had left

the vicinity of the door she threw herself down on a couch and burst into tears, exclaiming softly to herself between the sobs:

"My Wat! my poor Wat! my darling child, is it come to this with you?"

Then after a while she dried her eyes and sat up. "Perhaps all may go well with him after all. Perhaps this venture of his may come right. It was lucky I got him out of the room so soon. Another moment and I should have broken down, and been more dramatic and Continental than he, and that would never do. No son respects or relies on a mother who weeps on his bosom, and causes him to remember she is not his earliest and strongest friend."

In the strong-room of the Daneford Bank all the money and securities held by the bank were kept. The last duty of Mr. Aldridge, manager of the Daneford

Bank, each day, was to return the cash,
bills, books, &c., to this strong-room. To
this strong-room there were three keys in
the possession of the staff of the bank,
one held by the manager, one by the
accountant, and one by the teller.

The door could not be opened save by
the aid of the three keys. Thus no officer
of the Bank could commit a larceny in
the strong-room without the countenance
of two others.

Mr. Grey had duplicates of the keys
held by the accountant and teller. But
the key held by the manager was
unique, and even Mr. Grey himself could
not enter the strong-room without the
manager's key.

In this strong-room were kept not only
the valuables of the bank, but cases and
chests containing all kinds of highly port-
able and extremely precious substances
and papers belonging to customers of the

Bank. Here were iron plate-chests, iron deed-boxes, jewel-caskets in great numbers, left for safe keeping, not being part of the Bank's property, and against which there was no charge by the Bank but an almost nominal one for storage.

The evening after Mr. Grey had that interview with his mother, he called at the Bank, found the manager in, and having told Mr. Aldridge that a secret report had reached him to the disadvantage of a customer whose name he was not allowed to disclose, he wished to borrow the manager's key for half an hour, as he wanted to turn over the suspected man's account.

He got the key and a candle, and went down to the strong-room. In half an hour he returned, and handing back the key to Mr. Aldridge, said: "I am glad to say that the account I spoke of is quite satisfactory, and that it will not be necessary to make any alteration in our dealings with the customer I alluded to."

The next day Mr. Grey went to London, and returned the evening after. A few days later, among the letters was an advice from Mr. Grey's London correspondents to the effect that Messrs. Barrington, Ware, & Duncan had lodged twenty thousand pounds with them to Mr. Grey's credit.

That day Mr. Grey called upon his mother, and told her some of the expected good luck had come — not all, but still twenty thousand out of the fire.

"I told you, Henry, you had only to wait and face it, and you would win. If you did any of those romantic and foolish things with daggers and poison-bowls, they would say you were little better than a thief."

"Now they could not even say as much," he said softly to himself.

"What *are* you dreaming about now!" his mother cried, in exasperation.

He looked up with one of his best and brightest smiles, and said: "Dreams, madam! nay, it is. I know not dreams;" and kissing his mother to punctuate his parody, he smiled again, and added: "I was only joking, just to enjoy the sight of your anger now that things are looking better. Good-bye."

And so he left her.

CHAPTER V.

THE city of Daneford, on the river Wees-lade, is about eighteen miles from the small watering-town, Seacliff, which stands in a little bay at the mouth of the river. Between Daneford and Seacliff the width of the river varies, but is never less than a mile.

At a distance of less than four miles from the city the river widens considerably into a loop, and in the loop is the island of Warfinger. The island, which rarely is called by its particular name, but is spoken of as "The Island," measures a mile long by half a mile broad. It rises gradually

from the shores to the centre, and on the
highest point of it stands Island Castle,
the seat of the Midharsts for generations.
In the neighbourhood the title of Island
Castle is cut down also, and no one at
all familiar with the locality ever calls it
anything but " The Castle."

In the early part of the year 1866
the tenant for life of Island Castle was
old Sir Alexander Midharst, a widower,
who lived in the Castle in great retirement and the meanest economy. His wife
had then been dead twenty years. She
had died in giving birth to her only
child, Maud, now rapidly approaching her
majority; a girl of such gentle beauty
and simple childlike manners that all who
met her spoke of her beauty and her
grace with tender respect and ready
enthusiasm.

Maud Midharst did not need any adven-
titious aid to make her beauty apparent

and her presence acceptable, but her deli-
cate complexion, her dark sweet eyes, her
pleasant smile, all came out in strong contrast with her surroundings at the Castle.

In the building everything, including
the structure itself, seemed hastening to
decay. The walls, the floor, the furniture,
the servants, the master, all were old.
She formed the one exception to the
general appearance of approaching dissolution. The outer walls of the pile
were seamed and lined, the water had
eaten into the stone, the frost had
cracked the mortar, and unsightly yellow
stains lay upon the masonry, like long
skeleton fingers pointing to the earth into
which the walls were hastening.

When castles were places of defence as
well as of residence, Island Castle was well
known. It had stood two sieges, and had
been a famous place of meeting among
the Jacobites. Its insular position, the

wide prospect it commanded, the fact
that it could not be invested on all sides
at once except by a whole army, the
facilities it afforded to approach and flight
of friends, and the difficulty, amounting
almost to an impossibility, of reaching it
by surprise except under the favour of
night or a fog, all added together made
it a place of great importance once upon
a time.

The Castle had not always been in
the Midharst family. It had come to
them early in the eighteenth century,
upon the failure in heirs male of the
great Fleurey family, by which failure the
historic earldom of Stancroft was lost to
the blood for ever. The Midharsts had
some of the female Fleurey blood in their
veins, but it was of distant origin ; and
title to the fine castle and property was
declared to Sir John Midharst, the first
of his name who laid claim to it, only

after long and expensive litigation and much scandal.

Up to that time the Midharsts had been poor baronets. The property accompanying the Island in the year 1866 brought in a rental of more than twenty-two thousand pounds a year.

It was a very singular fact that from the first baronet who sat as master in Warfinger Island Castle down to old Sir Alexander, no son succeeded a father. It was always a grandson or a nephew, or a grand-nephew or some remote cousin. Now matters were worse than ever. Sir Alexander was upwards of seventy years of age, with an only child, a daughter, and the closest male was a direct descendant of the youngest son of the baronet, the lucky Sir John who came in for the property that had supported the extinct earldom of Stancroft.

No doubt this remote cousin was a

Midharst in name and blood, but some-
how it was hard for Sir Alexander to
feel very cordial or friendly towards one
so remote from him, one who was going
to take the property and the title away
from his immediate family.

At the time Lady Midharst died Sir
Alexander was but a little over fifty years
of age, and many thought he would marry
again. But even then he was ailing, and
doctors told him that between asthma and
valvular derangement of the heart his
chance of living even a few years was
slight. Of course, they said, he might
live fifty years, but he was heavily
handicapped.

As long as his wife, who had been
much younger than he, lived he continued
to hope for an heir; but upon the death
of Lady Midharst, having ascertained the
precise nature and import of the diseases
from which he suffered, he made up his

mind to give up all thought of an heir, and devote himself wholly to making a suitable provision for his daughter Maud, who was healthy and well-grown, and promised to be strong and long-lived.

And now began with Sir Alexander Midharst the practices by which he disgraced his order, and made himself a byword for all who knew his habits and his name.

He shut up his London house and advertised it to be let. A rich distiller took it furnished at two hundred pounds a month during the season, and a manufacturing jeweller for eighty pounds a month during the unfashionable periods of the year.

He sold his horses and carriages, all save one old state coach, which he could not sell for two reasons; first, because its preservation and " maintenance " were provided for by his predecessors; and secondly, because no one would pay haulage for it from the Island to the city.

He dismissed all his servants but the housekeeper, one maid, and one man, allowing, however, a nurse and "governess" for the baby, who yet lacked of three months. He resigned the membership of his two London clubs, of the three county clubs he belonged to, and intimated to all institutions or bodies or guilds to which he was patron, chairman, subscriber, or member, that his connection in any way with them must cease.

He discharged his steward, and resolved upon collecting his own rents and superintending his own property.

Up to this anyone who chose might go over his fine old Castle. Anyone still might go over the Castle, but an entrance fee of one shilling was now demanded from each sightseer.

As time advanced, and he became more imbued with avarice, more expert in meanness, he cut and shaved and clipped here and there and everywhere, until he had reduced his expenditure to about a thousand a year.

But he did not rest content with cutting down his own expenses; he was fully as careful to increase his income by every means in his power.

When leases expired they were renewed only on payment of heavy fines. His care was not so much to inflate the rent-roll as to get in all the ready-money he could. He had, he calculated, only a few years, if so long, to live, and the rent-roll would then be the concern of that William Midharst whom he had never seen and whom he wished never to see.

He cut down and sold all the timber as far as his right to do so extended; and all the trimming and underwood,

which had previously been allowed to go
as perquisites to the men or as gleaning
among the poor, he took possession of
and sold.

He let the right of shooting over
his land and the right of fishing in his
streams and rivers. He sold off all he
might of the more modern furniture at
the Castle.

He sold all his personal plate and
jewels, and all the pictures he had
acquired in his lifetime. When he was
young he had made a collection of coins ;
this, too, he converted into cash.

At one time he contemplated letting
one wing of the Castle to a rich tallow-
chandler of the city, and was absolutely
in treaty with him, when with a shudder
of shame he drew back and broke off
the negotiations.

When he commenced his scheme of
economy and exactions, he had said to

himself that if he pursued it for one
year, and sold off all the things he then
contemplated, he should be able to leave
his baby-girl close on forty thousand
pounds. At the end of twelve months
he found he had put more money together
than he had anticipated. There was no
new cause of anxiety with regard to his
health, and he made up his mind to
continue upon the track he had adopted.
He might live a year, ay, two years yet;
if he lasted two years more the leases of
Garfield estate would fall in, and he should
reap a harvest out of renewals. Give
him two years more, that is, three from
the beginning, and he should be able
to leave his only child close upon one
hundred thousand pounds.

At the end of the three years he
found he had not come within several
thousand pounds of his limit; so he resolved to complete the hundred thousand

before˺ he changed his manner of living or of dealing with the property.

When the end of the fourth year was reached he had saved more than the hundred thousand pounds. By this time he had become accustomed to the loss of all his old associations, had grown to love the new, and, above all, had become the slave of avarice, that most inflexible and enduring of all the passions. Therefore, he threw all idea of change to the winds, and resolved as long as he lived, whether for a week or twenty years, to save all the money he could, in order that the descendants of his side of the family might be able to hold up their heads hereafter.

At the death of his wife Sir Alexander Midharst closed his London banking account and transferred all his business to the Daneford Bank, where he had had an account when he came into the property, and where his predecessor in the title had also kept his account.

Now in money matters Sir Alexander may have been a good sergeant, or even on occasions a trustworthy captain; but he was no general, and he knew it. He accordingly resolved to consult with Mr. Grey, father of Wat. He explained the whole scheme to the banker, and the purpose for which the money was being saved, and said that in the first place he wanted to invest the money safely, and in the second of course he wanted some interest for it.

The banker suggested that for the present the money should be invested in the Three per Cent. Consols, which could be realised readily should any more desirable form of investment offer itself, and where it would be as safe as in land.

After some consideration Sir Alexander

agreed to follow the banker's advice, on the condition that Mr. Grey would buy the stock, keep the account of it, with the heirloom jewels and plate of Island Castle, but that in this case Mr. Grey was to retain the key of the chest containing the valuables and transact all the business connected with the Consols, such as receiving dividends, crediting the amount, and buying in more Consols with the interest of the Consols themselves, and any money Sir Alexander should lodge to the Midharst (Consols) account.

"I shall save the money," said the baronet, "and you will take care of it."

And so it was arranged. Sir Alexander gave the banker power-of-attorney with regard to these Consols and all the money lodged to their account for the future; all communications from the Bank of England, of solicitors, or anyone else, were to be

addressed to Sir Alexander Midharst, Daneford Bank, Daneford. These letters were
to be opened and attended to by Mr. Grey,
who was to make a reasonable charge for
the trouble.

Things went on thus until the elder
Mr. Grey's death, when the son succeeded
to the banking business and a considerable
private fortune in 1856.

Young Mr. Grey, as soon as he came
into the business, at once waited upon Sir
Alexander Midharst, and said he would
advise that some new plan should be
adopted with regard to the baronet's
business and accounts.

The baronet, who knew young Grey
very well, and liked him exceedingly, told
him that his father had managed the business excellently, and that the son ought
to be able to do as well.

Young Grey said the responsibility was
very great, the sum being now more than

two hundred thousand pounds over which Grey had complete power.

The baronet took him by the hand and said :

"You are a younger man than your father, and ought not to be more timid. Our family have known your bank before now; for my part, I am not able to take charge of these things. I prefer your guardianship to that of my lawyer's or of anybody else. If your father charged too little for the trouble, you may charge more. You know the money is for my little daughter : the estates go to a stranger after my death ; and this money is the fortune of my child, that no man shall say she, a Midharst—the last of the direct line, I may say—was left penniless and portionless, though she may be left homeless, on the world."

"As you put it now I cannot refuse," answered young Grey.

"Look around you." They were in the gateway leading to the court-yard, with their faces turned towards the slope of the hill. "Look around you. I have shorn the land close for my child. I work night and day for her, as though her daily bread depended on my arms and my brain. I may die any time. I have no friend, no relative. I am alone with my child. Everyone seems against me. That greedy, rapacious young scoundrel who is to follow me is looking with hungry eyes upon Warfinger Island, and nightly praying for my death. All my old friends have given me up. I am not of them now, because I have striven to make provision for my child. They call me a sordid miser, a stain upon the order I share with them. Let them rave. I will do what I think right by my child. Let them do as they choose. I do not ask their help. I only ask them to let me alone. But you I ask

to help me; and you will, for you are not
ennobled by the accident of your birth, but
by the generosity of your nature."

If any power of wavering had remained
in young Grey, this appeal would have
overcome it. So the matter was finally
settled: the son was to act for the baronet
precisely as the father had acted before.

During the year 1856 Mr. Grey the
younger was a frequent visitor to Island
Castle. He liked boating; and often in
the fine evenings pulled down the river
Weeslade to the Island, had a consultation
with Sir Alexander, and then pulled back
to Daneford in the sweet fresh twilight.

Often when it was growing dusk, and
he was about to start from the Island for
the city, he pushed off his boat into mid-
stream, and rested on his oars, looking
up at the mouldering Castle standing out
clear against the darkening sky.

There was something desolate and

forlorn about that vast pile, inhabited by that ageing man and that young girl.

In front, facing the wider water-passage, it stood high above him, its blind gateway looking down upon him, a lonely round tower at the right of the archway catching the strange gleams of light reflected from the Weeslade as the river glided silently towards the sea.

Winter and summer, when there was sunshine at sunset, the top of that tower caught the reflection of the last red streak that flickered on the polished surface of the river. This fact affected long ago the superstitious feelings of the people. There was a tradition in the neighbourhood that in times gone by the wicked mother of a Lord Stancroft used abominable witchcraft against her daughter-in-law, her son's bride, newly brought home from the kingdom of Spain, a country far away, and near the sun, and full of gallant men and fine ladies, whose eyes it were a marvellous fine feast to see, but who were—the ladies —treacherous and light of love.

The abominable and damnable exercises practised by the wicked dowager caused the dark-eyed Lady Stancroft, who had come among strangers out of the far-away kingdom of Spain, to wither up and grow old and loathsome in a year. So that the young lord turned away from her, and cared nothing for her any more. And the poor young lady, gap-toothed and wrinkled and foul-looking as she had been made by devilish witchcraft, was still young in her mind and her affections, and doated on the lord, who would not as much as come nigh the Castle while she was there, but took to wine and evil ways.

So at last the poor young wife, who looked eighty, was lost, and could be found nowhere. It was long after, and in the time of the next lord, that, in the topmost

chamber of the round gate-tower, a chamber
never used save in war-time, they discovered
the skeleton of the young wife, and words
written in a strange tongue, the language
of Spain, saying how she had stolen up
there to die, as she could not win back
the love of her husband, the young lord.
Ever after that the topmost chamber of
the tower was red at sunset. Some
thought this red gleam came from the fire
where the wicked dowager Lady Stancroft
suffered for her great sin ; others thought
this was the reflection from the wreath
of glory worn by the poor young wife.
But all agreed it had to do with the deed
of the wicked Lady Stancroft ; and so
they called the tower the Witch's Tower,
a name it bore until Walter Grey gave it
another.

The year 1856 was one full of remarkable events in the life of Mr. Grey. In
it his father died ; he came into a con-

siderable fortune ; he purchased a house ;
and grew to be a frequent visitor at Island
Castle.   It often struck him as a peculiar
coincidence that in the same year he should
have become owner of the most remarkable
house near Daneford, and caretaker to the
fortune of the owner of the most remarkable
house in the whole district.

About that time he read an account
of a certain tree said to be in sympathy
with a certain tower.   The idea was fresh
to him, and seemed to open up a new field
of speculation, and he dwelt upon it a
good deal.

One evening, as he was rowing from
the Castle to his own home, a thought
flashed into his mind.   There was a striking coincidence in the fact of his being
connected so closely with two such houses.
Each was unpopular, each was weird,
strange ; there were queer stories about
each, each had a tower.   The tower of

one had an unpleasant history connected with the skeleton of that poor Spanish lady ; the tower on his house had that rusty framework of a tank that looked like a skeleton. " Might not," he thought, with a smile at the absurdity, " there be some sympathy between these two houses ? "

He ceased to row, and looked at the vast pile that brooded over the dark waters of the Weeslade. He rested upon his oars.

" It looks, if like anything human, like a witch charming the river. My house, too, looks like a witch sitting at bay within her magic circle of grove. It wouldn't be bad to name them both The Weird Sisters. They are uglier than the crones in ' Macbeth.' "

He pulled a few strokes and mused again, resting on his oars.

" They don't use that tower. I don't

use my tower. They found the skeleton of the Spanish Lady Stancroft in the top of that tower. There's the skeleton of that old tank on the top of mine. Towers and skeletons suggest Bombay and the Parsees. By Jove, the Towers of Silence would not be a bad name for those two."

Next day he told several people the names he had given the two houses and the two towers. All who heard of the new nomenclature smiled, and admired the cleverness; and from that time forth in Daneford the two houses were known as the Weird Sisters, and the two towers as the Towers of Silence.

CHAPTER VI.

"TO THE ISLAND OR TO——."

EARLY in the year 1866 the Midharst (Consols) account-book with the Daneford Bank showed that, after deducting all charges and paying all expenses, the principal and interest reached the enormous sum of five hundred and fifty thousand pounds, enough to buy such a property as the old baronet enjoyed.

By this time Sir Alexander had passed out of middle life into age. He was now thin and bent to one side, and very weak, but still firm of purpose. He had defeated the doctors by living so long;

he had defeated "that ungrateful whelp,"
as he called his heir-presumptive. Of this
distant cousin he had no knowledge whatever; he declined to listen to anything
about him. Why he called him ungrateful
no one ever knew; he called him a whelp
because he was young. It was believed
that Sir Alexander had never in all his
life set eyes upon him, or even got an
account of the young man from one who
knew him.

At the time of his wife's death, the
baronet made outline enquiries through
his solicitor as to the age and descent
of the boy. In the year of Lady
Midharst's death, the boy, whose father
had been a poor naval officer, was aged
eight, having been born in 1838. The
boy's father had died at sea. There
could not be the shadow of a doubt
that this William Midharst was heir -
presumptive, and, if he lived, would

inherit the title and the property, should Sir Alexander die without leaving a son.

Little of the baronet's time was spent with his daughter ; often a whole week went by, and he did not pass more than an hour of the whole time with her. She had a suite of rooms for herself, where she lived with Mrs. Grant, an officer's widow, who knew much of the world, and was now glad to accept the position of lady's companion to the baronet's only child.

Owing to the eccentric life led by Sir Alexander, the facts that he saw no company and had no intercourse with any of the county families, Maud never went into society, and was wholly dependent on good sympathetic little Mrs. Grant for any knowledge she might gain of the great outside world. Mrs. Grant, who was of a gay and pleasure-loving disposition, had no patience with the whims and meannesses of the old man.

"You know, my dear," she said to Maud, as they sat over their tea in Maud's little drawing-room, "it's all very well for Sir Alexander to go on saving up money for you, so that you may be a great heiress one of these days; but that isn't all. He treats you as if you were a girl of twelve yet. Why, my dear, I had been out three years before I was your age, and had refused three or four offers. I had, indeed. I know you don't want offers, my dear; but I did; for I was only a poor rector's daughter, and hadn't even beauty to help me."

"Indeed I am sure you must have been wonderfully pretty. You don't know now nice you look now," replied the girl softly.

"Ah, well, my dear, after a few seasons you get to know all about your good looks; and then, my dear, after a few seasons more you get to know what is of a great deal more consequence, all your defects, or at least a good many. I don't suppose any woman ever found out all the weak points in her appearance, and that's a mercy. But as I was saying—what was I saying?"

"I think," said Maud, with an expression of great innocence, "that you were blaming papa for never having given me an opportunity of finding out the weak points in my personal appearance."

"Yes, that's it. That is, not quite it. Maud, I won't have you twist things I say in that way. You know I am always for your good; indeed I am."

"I am quite sure of it, dear Mrs. Grant," returned the girl gratefully, and with a trace of moisture in her large soft eyes, as though she relented having taken advantage of the other's impetuosity.

The woman took her hand, and stroked it briskly, and said :

"There, there, Maud, don't be silly. Look at this very case in point. Why, you turn sentimental over a few words from an uninteresting middle-aged woman ! Now is that a proper thing in an heiress of twenty ? Why, my dear, you'd have no account to give of offers refused if once *you* went out. You'd marry the first booby who asked you, rather than disoblige him or cause him pain."

"I shall never marry anyone I do not love," said Maud, with an air of quiet decision.

"Maud, be silent; you are only a school-girl, with a lot of sound rules in your head, and not the least idea of how they are applied, or where. I tell you *I* know something of the world and girls and love and marriage. I tell you,

you'd marry the first stupid lout who said to you: 'Maud, I love you!'"

"Was the first who proposed to you a stupid lout?" asked the girl simply.

"No, he wasn't; at least I did think he was then, but I afterwards knew that he was the best of them all; and I was often sorry I did not take him."

"And did he marry?"

"Yes; he married a fool."

"Who had just come out — her first season?" asked Maud, with her hands folded serenely on her lap.

"Yes. But how did you guess?"

"Well, you see, you told me I should marry the first stupid lout who asked me, and I thought it likely a girl only just out did marry the stupid lout who proposed first to you."

"But, dear, I told you he wasn't a stupid lout; then I thought he was stupid, and was often sorry afterwards—of course I mean before I married—that I did not accept him."

"This gives me more hope for my own case. You see, the girl who had only just come out took the man you thought was a stupid lout, and was right in taking him."

Maud looked up and smiled.

For a moment Mrs. Grant tapped her foot impatiently on the carpet; looked hither and thither, rose a little hastily, and cried: "Well, Maud, if you don't think I have a very serious interest in what I say, I will say——" She paused, and looked at the sweet, half-frightened face of the girl. All at once her manner underwent a change. She drew near the girl, and putting her arm round her waist, "I will say," she continued, "that whoever gets you cannot help loving you. Men are often bad, Maud darling; but I don't think there is one such a villain and a fool as to be unkind to you."

As April of 1866 grew into May, the asthmatic affection from which the old baronet suffered abated; but the valvular defect of heart increased. He had fainted three or four times in the month of April, and in May his debility became so great that he was unable to leave his bed. Other symptoms now showed themselves, and complicated the case, and so embarrassed the action of the heart that the doctors declared he must expect a speedy termination. Towards the end of May the doctors declared he would never rise from his bed.

The old man, whose spirit was in arms against these doctors, would not believe them. Twenty years ago they had told him the same thing.

They said : No, the circumstances were different. They had then said he *might*

go at any moment; things were worse
than that now. There was no longer
any chance of recovery, and the dread
was things would grow worse.

The doctors found it necessary to be
almost brutally candid with him, for they
had learned he had not yet made his
will.

Insecure as was the tenure upon which
he had for the past twenty years held
his life, he had gone on from day to day
deferring the arrangement of his affairs
on the grounds that he was too busy,
and that if he made his will now he
should have to add codicils according
as his savings increased. His lawyer
assured him no such thing was necessary, because, after all bequests had been
mentioned, he could leave his daughter
residuary legatee absolutely or with any
provisions and restrictions he liked to
impose.

As the lawyer had failed in the old
time the doctors failed now. But they
were resolved to leave no stone unturned
in their attempt to get him to settle his
affairs. The dying man's daughter was
too young, and too timid, and too closely
interested in the execution of the document to think of asking her aid; so
they resolved to summon Mrs. Grant, and
request her to press the matter home to
the mind of the invalid.

In the great banqueting-room the three
physicians in attendance sat when it was
resolved to invoke Mrs. Grant.

The vast apartment had been allowed
to fall almost into ruins. It was the
finest room in the house, and few houses
in either county that claimed the banks
of the Weeslade at this point could boast
so noble a chamber.

But twenty years of neglect had defiled
and defaced the room. The curtains were

faded and worn, the hair grinned through the torn covers of the fine old oak chairs. Damp had attacked the moulding of the picture frames, and here and there the moulding had fallen off, leaving the bones of the discoloured frames exposed to view. The ceiling, formed of oak cross-beams, with flowers and fruit pieces in the panels, had felt the corroding touch of wilful Time. Here and there the canvas bulged off the panel, and hung in loose flabby blisters from the roof. The fine oak floor had grown dull and woolly for want of use and care. Sir Alexander kept no servants to look after the apartments he did not make use of, and refused to allow even beeswax for the floors.

The dog-irons, which had stood watch over the home-fire of generations of his name and blood, were rusted. The tapestries hanging across the doors, here and there torn from their hooks, hung in neglected disorder from the rods. The hospitable greeting "Welcome," in blue enamel in the wreath of carved vine-leaves round the top of the huge sideboard, had lost some of its letters. The glasses of the lamps held by the bronze Nubian slaves at the doors were reduced to half their number. The leather thongs lacing the suits of armour that held the groups of candles at either end of the sideboard had rotted and parted, and the helmets and back and breast plates gaped at the sutures.

The chamber smelt like a vault just opened, and, although the weather was bright and fine, all the furniture, the walls, the floor, felt damp and slimy.

As soon as the doctors had finished luncheon, Mrs. Grant was sent for. She arrived in a state of great agitation; she feared that Sir Alexander was in the last extremity.

Dr. Hardy, the senior physician, a pale, soft-voiced, self-contained man of few words, was the spokesman. He said:

"You will be glad to hear, and you will be kind enough to inform Miss Midharst, that there is no cause for any alarm on account of the present condition of Sir Alexander."

Mrs. Grant looked infinitely relieved. Strange and unsympathetic a father as the invalid had been, she did not like the thought of having to tell anything dreadful about him to Maud.

"I am glad to hear it. Shall I go at once and tell Miss Midharst the good news?"

Dr. Hardy held up his hand with a gesture which said quite plainly: "If you will be so kind as to confine your attention to me, you may rest assured of knowing explicitly what I wish to have done in this matter." Having allowed the gesture

a little while to sink into the mind of
Mrs. Grant, he went on with his lips :

"*But,*" he said, with strong emphasis
on the conjunction, to show Mrs. Grant
that she had interrupted him, and that
he regarded the interruption as frivolous,
"the case has now arrived at that state
of progress when almost at any time the
patient's head may be attacked. Should
the head be attacked, Sir Alexander will
lose the possession of those mental gifts
and powers which he now possesses un-
diminished and unimpaired."

"Poor child !" cried the widow, thinking
of the guileless daughter of the stricken
man.

"*And,*" continued Dr. Hardy, with the
same resolute emphasis on the conjunction, "we consider that he should be
at once induced to make his will, and
we have resolved to request you will
use your influence with him. We have

tried and failed. May we count on you ?"

Mrs. Grant looked up with a half-amused, half-astonished air. As soon as she had somewhat recovered from her surprise, she said very earnestly :

"There is nothing in this world I would not try to do for Miss Midharst; but there is no more chance of Sir Alexander listening to me on any business matter than of his asking advice of the wind. He believes women can and ought to know nothing about business. It would only vex him if I spoke of anything of the kind to him."

The poor little woman looked quite distressed and helpless.

The three men glanced from one to the other in despair. In a few seconds Dr. Hardy spoke again to the little widow.

" Is there no friend of the patient's

whom you could suggest as likely to
have influence on him? Do you think
his lawyer would have weight? We
know how he has secluded himself from
the world and his own class, and that
we are not to look among those who
would naturally be his friends for the
assistance we now want. Do you think
his lawyer would be likely to succeed
with him in this?"

"I am greatly afraid not. I have
heard that — although he has a high
opinion of Mr. Shaw, his lawyer — he
would never in any way accept advice
in his affairs beyond legal matters. I
understand Sir Alexander has no personal liking for Mr. Shaw. And he
won't speak to any clergyman."

Again the three men looked at one
another in doubt and difficulty. Again
Dr. Hardy spoke:

"This is a matter of the utmost

importance to those who come after Sir Alexander, and we are most anxious it should be settled, and at once. If we thought it was a disinclination to make a will, or a determination not to make one, that kept him back, we should feel no responsibility in the matter. But he refuses to settle his worldly affairs solely upon the ground that we are deceived as to his condition of health. Now we are confident we are right. He will never rise from his bed again. Already dropsy has made its appearance; at any moment that may, directly or indirectly, affect the head; in his case it is almost sure to do so at some time."

Dr. Hardy paused a moment; then proceeded with more decision than heretofore :

" Perhaps you, Mrs. Grant, would be kind enough to ask Miss Midharst if she could give you the name of anyone on whose advice Sir Alexander would be likely to rely in an important business affair? You need not distress Miss Midharst with anything more explicit."

Mrs. Grant rose with prompt willingness, and hurried away in the sustaining hope that Maud might be able to solve the difficulty.

When Mrs. Grant had gone, the three men drew near one of the tall narrow windows that looked west along the Island and commanded the beautiful valley of the broad river, and the broad, blue, bright Weeslade itself.

An everlasting Sabbath filled that luxuriant valley with a peace which seemed too fine for earth. Because of the height on which the Castle stood, and its distance from the nearest shore beyond the western end of the Island, all detail was subdued and lost; nothing was left to trouble the eye or excite enquiry. The eye could see nothing but broad green pasturages and vast expanses of emerald grainshoots reaching down to the river's brink, and sloping softly inward towards the quiet hills that stood up apart, clad in purple and blue wood, and crowned with violet uplands lying secure against the azure sky.

The tide was full; the winds were still; from the trees around through the open window came the fragrant spices of the may. Above, the lark took up where all human voices end the praises of the spring. The glory of inextinguishable youth was in his song, the wild rapture of a regenerated soul. Below, the sad-throated thrush piped of the mellow melancholy of a ripe old world that had borne a thousand generations of men, who had moved all their days through the same narrow and unsatisfying avenues of desire and passion and fina failure to the richly padded grave. The thrush sang to the earth of those who had died ; the lark sang to the skies of those who shall live for ever.

Around the three men as they stood by the open window was the mouldering chamber of an ancient house. On one side lay the decayed old man of a noble race. On the other side the maiden daughter of that man, who had smothered up his affectionate visitings under piles of gold, scraped together for her, for the pride of his lineage.

Beyond there in the city was ruin. A great bank which had a branch in Daneford had stopped payment to-day. The three men by the window were talking of that while they awaited the return of the woman.

"Dreadful ! I am told that the poor Mainwarings are completely ruined by it."

"Completely. Fancy old John Musgrave put four thousand pounds into it on deposit this day week. It will kill him. He had sold out Turks, and was going to buy United States."

"Poor old fellow! I do pity him."

"There was a rumour of one of the local banks being in a bad way. Did either of you hear it?"

"Not the Daneford?"

"No; Grey is safe. Bless me, his father left him a couple of hundred thousand clear of the business, and he's been making money ever since."

"Is it the Weeslade Valley?"

"I don't like to say. It is so dangerous to speak. But there *is* a rumour of a local bank, and it's *not Grey's.*"

"No. I should think Grey could stand anything. They say it was always Grey's system to keep the money near home. It's a commercial and customers' bank, and not a gad-about among foreign speculations and bubble manufacturers."

At that moment Mrs. Grant re-entered the room.

The three men turned round and went to her.

"I have seen Miss Midharst, and she says she thinks the person most likely to have influence with Sir Alexander is Mr. Grey the banker."

"A most excellent man," said Dr. Hardy, turning to the other two. "What do you think?"

"Capital!"

"No one could be better."

Dr. Hardy spoke to Mrs. Grant for the last time on that occasion. "Send a note by express to Mr. Grey, requesting him to come immediately. Explain to him what our views are, and ask him to do his best to induce Sir Alexander to make his will."

In less than an hour and a half Mr. Grey received Mrs. Grant's letter. It merely said that his presence was urgently desired at the Castle at once, and that by hurrying he would greatly oblige Sarah Grant.

He was in his private room at the Bank when he read the letter. He opened his private black bag. Bank proprietors do not always carry firearms, in fact rarely, almost never. Clerks in charge of money often do. Grey always carried a revolver—now.

"He can't have heard of his Consols? In that case he would have written himself or come. What can this be?—so sudden, so urgent, and from Mrs. Grant! Perhaps the failure of the St. George's has frightened him. If he asks me to give up the money now! Ah, I can't face that! No, no! This first," and he took a revolver out of his bag.

Again he thought awhile, and ended with a question: "Shall I go to the Island or to——?" He poised the revolver.

As he did so there was a knock at the door.

CHAPTER VII.

TRUSTEE TO CANCELLED PAGES.

"COME in," said the banker mechanically, and his mother entered.

With a start Mr. Grey's mother cried out "Henry!" then crossed the room hastily, and, putting her hand on his arm, looked up into his face with alarm.

With an amused smile he glanced down at her, and said simply, "Mother?" in a tone of badinage, as if paying her off in her own coin by replying to her with a single word.

"What was that you held in your hand and dropped into the bag as I came in?" she asked with reproachful earnestness, looking up fixedly into his eyes, as though she would pierce to his innermost thoughts.

He put his hand on her shoulder playfully, and smoothed one of the black silk strings of her black bonnet with his thumb and finger, returning her steady gaze with a steady eye and a free smile. "That, mother," he answered, " is the countersign for thieves."

" The countersign for thieves! What do you mean, Henry ; you ought not to bandy words with your mother."

"Indeed, I am not playing with words. I am only describing the weapon and its use as briefly as possible. I was looking at my revolver, for I was just about to set out on a journey. You see, if a thief comes up to a man armed with a revolver, and demands the man's purse, the man produces that revolver, and the thief says, "Pass on, friend." If a thief who has stolen money meets the man he stole it from, or a policeman, and can pull out a revolver, then he can say to the man or the policeman, "Let me pass, or I will shoot you down;" or suppose the thief finds the odds are against him, he can put the barrel to his own temple, and pass the foe in spite of numbers. Now, mother, don't you think my explanation is very clever and very exhaustive?"

He placed his two hands on the widow's shoulders, and pushed her back arm's length, dropped his head roguishly over his shoulder, and laughed a soft laugh, which seemed to invite her to enjoy his cleverness and be amused at the humour of the explanation.

Mrs. Grey did not smile. For a moment her face grew puckered and perplexed. In her eyes shone the light of a mental conflict between anger and tears. The conflict ended in a few moments. She threw herself into a chair and covered her face with her hands. She neither stormed nor wept.

He hastened to her with compunctious solicitude. He knelt on one knee by her side, and put his powerful arm round her emaciated shoulders, and with the hand of his other arm gently drew down her hands from her face.

" Mother ! mother ! " he pleaded, in a tone of passionate tenderness. " I did not mean to annoy or trouble you. I was only a little wilfully following out a fancy, a conceit. It was a foolish vanity that made me seem to play with your questions. You know, my own mother, I would not give you any pain I could help, for all the world. Forgive me, and let us drop the nonsense. Forgive me, and let us speak of something else."

All the earnestness of this man's nature went into these words, and there was in them and the manner attending them a fervid pathos which stirred the heart of the woman so deeply it almost killed her to keep from crying out, and throwing her arms round her son, and weeping on his breast. But by a superhuman effort, an effort no created being could make but a mother for the salvation of a child, she held her passionate love within her own heart; for, according to her theory, so must all women who wish to rule their children; and she wanted to rule, not for the love of power, but for the love of love and the preservation of her son.

She gave one quick glance at him out of those sharp eyes, and then throwing down the eyes on the ground, said in a constrained voice:

"The St. George's Banking Company

has failed. There is a run on the Daneford. You are unable to meet that run, and you were thinking of getting away from the run and the closing of the doors with—— that." She shuddered, raised her hand, and pointed to the black bag into which he had dropped the revolver.

"No! no! no! mother!" he cried imploringly. "I pledge you my word— if you like I will prove to you—that we are able to meet any run that may come upon us in consequence of this failure. If you like I will call in Aldridge to corroborate my words."

"Corroborate your word, Henry!" she cried scornfully. "Do you think I could doubt my son's word, and believe the word of any other man alive! Never while I live, I hope, shall you fall so pitifully low as to need another man's word to help your word to my belief." She laid hold of the imputed question of her son's word as a point on which to rally her disordered feelings and overcome the tendency she felt to break down.

"Well, mother, rest assured this run threatens us with no danger whatever. On the contrary, as we are able to meet it without the least inconvenience, the position of the Bank ought to be very materially improved when all becomes quiet again." He rose and left her as he spoke, and locked the two doors of the room, observing: "We don't want anyone to come in and interrupt us now."

By the time he returned to his seat she had recovered her composure. "Then what do you mean by 'setting out on a journey?' Those words helped me into the fear."

As a reply to that question, he pushed the note he had just received from Mrs. Grant across the table to her,.

and said : " Read that, and you will understand."

She adjusted her tortoiseshell spectacles and read the note deliberately. When she had finished she looked up quickly.

He was standing at the window looking out. His back was towards her, and she could not see his face. It was wrinkled and drawn up like a yellow leaf.

" Do you know what you are wanted for at the Castle ?" she asked briskly.

" No."

" What has happened to your voice ?" she asked, in a tone of anxiety and surprise. He had spoken as though his windpipe was almost closed in a gripe.

" Nothing ; or at least something has gone against my—breath. What am I wanted for at the Castle ? " Still he spoke as if half suffocated. Still he kept

his face to the window. Still his face
was wrinkled and yellow and withered
up.

"I met Dr. Hardy as I came in. He
had just driven straight back from the
Castle. There has been a consultation
of doctors to-day, and they have little or
no hope of Sir Alexander getting better.
He has not yet made his will, and they
all agreed you were the only person
likely to have any influence with him.
They could get him to do nothing about
it."

Grey's face cleared as if by magic.
He turned round suddenly, threw up
both his hands, and burst into a loud
and continuous shout of laughter.

His mother started to her feet, and
looked at him aghast. "Henry!" she
cried, in great alarm; "Henry, what is
the matter?"

"Nothing, mother, nothing," he said

between his laughter; "I thought it was something serious."

She regarded him in a stupor of amazement for a few seconds. "You thought it was something serious," she whispered, as if she questioned her hearing.

"Yes, something very serious."

"But it is very serious. He is in danger of death, and has not yet made his will. Surely that, Henry, is no subject for laughter."

He was composed now. His face was radiant, and he smiled apologetically as he said: "You must really forgive me, dear mother. The fact is, for the past quarter of an hour I have been on such a stretch in the interview between us that to hear of anything else but my own affairs relieved me, and I could not help laughing. I did not, indeed, laugh at the thought of poor Sir Alexander being ill;

I pity him with all my heart. But what you said touched some spring of my mind, and I could no more have forborne to laugh than to breathe for an hour. Well, I think I had better start for the Island at once. You now feel all right about the Bank? You feel quite comfortable about it, mother, don't you?"

"Yes, but do not be so odd, Henry; you frighten me to death with your strange ways of late."

"I have a good deal of anxiety, and perhaps am too abrupt. More of my abruptness: I can't wait another moment. Good-bye, mother."

And in a few seconds he had gone.

When she found herself alone, she sat down to recover and to reflect. "Every day," she thought, "he becomes less like his old self, and more of a riddle."

Her eyes caught something on the table.

"When I came in he told me he was

examining that dreadful thing because he was going on a journey, and now he's gone off and left it behind him in the bag on that table. Can it be he is losing his reason ?"

When Mr. Grey found himself outside the Bank-door he hailed the nearest fly, jumped in, and cried cheerily to the driver :

"Island Ferry, and I lay you a half-crown to a whip-lash you don't do it under half an hour. Take the time and drive on."

With a chuckle of grave satisfaction, the banker threw himself back in the fly, and as they drove rapidly through the town he waved his hand or doffed his hat at every twenty yards. There was cordiality in every look that greeted him, and many who saw him go by turned and gazed with admiration and envy after the fine rich jovial banker.

No wonder he looked pleased. An hour ago, less than an hour ago, he had, upon reading that note, almost come to the conclusion Sir Alexander Midharst had discovered he, Grey, had "borrowed" every penny of the immense sum confided to his charge by the baronet. Such a discovery would have been to him simply and literally fatal.

Early in this year, when he disclosed the secret of the Bank to his mother, he and it were bankrupt, and all the depositors' money was gone. Pressure after pressure had come upon him after that, and all such demands had been met by "borrowing" the baronet's savings without the baronet's consent.

Three months ago he was a bankrupt, now he was a bankrupt and a thief. He had no more right to sell those Consols than to put his hand into any customer's pocket and take his purse. He had

glided into the thing gradually, beginning
by borrowing twenty thousand pounds,
which he caused to be lodged to his own
credit at his London agents in the name
of Barrington, Ware, and Duncan, an
imaginary firm of Boston merchants, who
remitted the money through their London
agent on account of supposititious dealings
in hides on the western coast of the
United States.

The twenty thousand had only stopped
the gap for a few days. Then heavier
and heavier bills came to maturity, and
before there was any general uneasiness
in the commercial world, one hundred
thousand pounds of the baronet's savings
had been " borrowed."

Then came ugly rumours of certain
banking establishments; and although the
Daneford Bank was always spoken of
with the highest esteem in the district,
the city, and in such quarters of London

as it was known, the accommodation market had got very much straitened, and the Daneford Bank's London agents not only hinted they did not care to make any additional advances, but sounded Grey as to the possibility of their being able to get a little advance from him. Could he let them have fifty thousand for six weeks on Argentines they did not want to sell?

Here was a chance of showing the stability of his own concern and helping a friendly firm which might be of incalculable use to him another time. Now that he had dipped into the Midharst fund, why not go deeper? He could make something out of this transaction; and it was for the good of Sir Alexander as well as himself that he should try to pull back all the money he could, and keep the name of the Bank at the very highest level. He lent the money.

Then came other pressures because of those old speculations, a quarter of million at least; and last, more uneasy rumours in the financial world, and the possibility of a run on the Bank. At all risks the Bank must stand; for on its stability depended not only the life of Henry Walter Grey, but all chance of winning back any portion of the baronet's money.

When the moment of this decision arrived Grey put down his last stake; sold the last hundred thousand of Sir Alexander's half a million Consols, and bought the revolver. As he put the matter to himself in his figurative way, the situation now was a race between gold and lead. Would the gold, in the form of profits and deposits, come back to him in such quantities as to prevent the necessity for the outgoing of the lead?

It was on Wednesday, the 30th of May, 1866, he got that note from Mrs.

Grant. He had just been calculating his chances of falling in for some of the business of the St. George's Bank. He had even put down a few figures to please and flatter his sight. It might be that if he could hold on and get — say, half the business of the Daneford branch of the St. George's Bank, the chance of the gold overtaking the lead would be enormously increased. All this was of course contingent upon Sir Alexander remaining in ignorance of the " borrowing." If that came to his ears in any way, nothing could prevent the lead overtaking the gold.

That note almost precipitated the crisis. In the usual way when he was wanted at the Castle Sir Alexander wrote a line himself, or called and asked the banker down for the evening. This note did not come from Sir Alexander, but from Miss Midharst's companion. At the moment when his mother entered a straw might have turned his resolution in favour of giving the lead a walk-over. But with the news brought by his mother all was changed, and the gold had taken a good lead.

As he sat back in the fly and reviewed his position he could hardly restrain his exultation within the bounds of mere facial joy. He would have liked to get out and run through the streets, and shout.

A few minutes ago he held all black cards to a red trump. Now the whole pack seemed to have been put before him face up, with liberty to select his own hand and turn a trump of his own choosing.

No run could injure the Daneford Bank; other banks might fail, but his was secure for the time ; and by the aid of its good substantial name the Daneford would get strong while others were crumbling, and the future success of the Bank would be assured beyond the reach of his highest hope of years ago.

Only two possible chances were against him, and if neither of these chances turned up within twelve months he might laugh at fate.

The former was that in the will there should be introduced anything adverse to him. The latter was that the old man should die in less than twelve months, and leave it incumbent on the banker to render an account and deliver up the money before the end of twelve months.

Grey had fully made up his mind as to the necessity for a will. Without a will there would in all likelihood be Chancery proceedings; and while no one in Daneford would dream of suspecting Grey, or ask details of the account, much less verification of the items, the Chancery folk will go through the whole affair as a matter of routine, and not as a matter of precaution, or because of any suspicion.

Let there be a will, by all means.

It was fine to drive through the bright sunlight of that glorious May weather, and feel that the gold was overtaking the lead. It was better than recovering from a long illness; it was coming back, to life and green fields and the voices of birds and the pressure of hands we love, out of the dark, damp, noisome tomb.

When Mr. Grey arrived at Island Ferry he alighted, told the driver of the fly to wait for him, and took the boat to the Island.

As soon as he arrived at the Castle he was shown into the dreary deserted banquet-room.

Here he found irrepressible little Mrs. Grant waiting for him. After some time he gathered from her how matters stood, and sent up his name to the sick man.

Sir Alexander would see Mr. Grey.

When the banker reached the room where the baronet lay, he was greatly shocked at the change which had taken place in the latter since the last time they had met, although that was only a few days ago.

There had always been a bright bloom, the bloom of old age heightened and deepened by the malady which afflicted him chronically, on the old man's face. Now the cheeks were puffed and purple, and the eyes, once so keen and cold, were dull and restless and impatient.

The long thin sinewy hands lay outside the counterpane, and the voice of the sufferer when he spoke was tremulous, querulous, making a painful contrast to the firm, clear, thin, biting speech of other days.

After the usual greetings and Grey's expression of sorrow for his indisposition, the old man spoke quickly, and in an unsteady voice.

" These doctors have been worrying me to-day, Grey, and I am very glad you have come. I want to talk to you. Pull that curtain a little across the window; I hate the sunlight. Thank you, Grey. Sit down now, where I can see you. It's a comfort to look at a man like you after those false prophets and hoarse ravens. The doctors have been with me, Grey; and they tell me I should make my will. Now I'm not talking to you as a medical man, but as a man of business. What do you say ?"

" Have you spoken to Mr. Shaw about the matter ?" asked the banker softly.

" No; I have not spoken to Shaw about it. I hate lawyers," cried the old man pettishly.

"If I hated lawyers," returned Grey, with a shy smile, "I should not be without a will for four-and-twenty hours."

"Why?" demanded the old man, with a contraction of the brows and a glance of suspicion directed at an imaginary group of lawyers.

"You know, Sir Alexander, lawyers have a special prayer, asking for the management of intestate estates." He raised his eyebrows and smiled archly at the prostrate man.

"I don't understand you, Grey. These doctors, with their fears and their jargon, have confused me. What do you mean?"

For a moment the banker looked at the baronet uneasily. Could it be that already his mind was becoming clouded or torpid? After a moment's observation and thought, Grey decided that the old man was only dazed and tired.

"What I mean, Sir Alexander, is, that

in cases where there is no will, the law-costs often consume the whole estate, and *always* eat up enormously more money than where there is a sound will."

The old man reflected awhile.

"Have you made your own will?" he asked.

"Certainly. I could not rest if I thought what little fortune I may have should, instead of going to my wife, be scattered about in this and that court, in this and that litigation. As I go home the ferry-boat may overturn and I may be drowned, the horse may run away and I may be killed. Making a will has with me no connection with good or bad health. It is a business thing which ought, on the principle of economy, to be done in time. In nothing more than in making a will is it true that a stitch in time saves nine?"

There was a long pause.

" Grey !"

" Yes, Sir Alexander."

" You helped me to put this fortune together for my daughter."

A bow of deprecation.

" You have been ten years now taking care of it for her."

" Yes, Sir Alexander." What was coming now? Could all this be a *ruse?* Was this serene interview to end in a storm of intolerable ruin? Had this old man been leading up with deceiving equanimity to some prodigious burst, some unendurable tempest of reproach?

" Will you go still farther ?"

" In what way ?"

" Will you act as one of the executors, the chief—no, as the sole, as sole trustee and guardian ?"

" What ! Sir Alexander, Sir Alexander, are you—are you trifling with me ? If you are, give it up. I cannot, I will not, be trifled with." His face shrivelled up, and he covered it in his hands. For that brief space he thought all had been discovered.

"What I say I mean. Why should I trifle with you? If I am to die or be killed, let me die with the knowledge that the fortune of my child will be as safe when I am dead as it is now. Will you do this, Grey, for me?"

"I will."

"Then you may tell Shaw to come. Go to him at once. I wish to make my will."

CHAPTER VIII.

WAT GREY'S ROMANCE DIES OUT.

MR. GREY'S drive to Castle Ferry had been an excursion to meet victory; his return to Daneford was a triumphant progress.

Now it seemed to him nothing short of a conspiracy between fate and accident could wreck him. The two chances which had threatened him with ruin had melted into thin air. Nothing adverse to him would be in the will, and not only that, but from the day of Sir Alexander's death until the coming of age of Miss Midharst he would have absolute control of affairs, and every chance of making good the sum he had abstracted. The gold was going to beat the lead at a walk.

The financial world was now in a state of deplorable despondency, but that condition of things could not last for ever. There was of course no prospect of his making a tenth part of the half a million profit during the twelve months; but the St. George's Bank was gone, and deposits would come flowing in, and having obliged his London agents in their need, they could not refuse him anything in reason by-and-by. After riding out the bad times his credit would be so firmly established that he could get money on the best terms to build up the horrible gap he had made. He could borrow to replace what he had stolen.

"I shall win now, and I shall win easily," he thought, as he drove through the bright fresh air towards Daneford; "and by the time there is another dissolution, who can tell but I may take one of the seats for the city, if it is offered to me."

He went straight to Mr. Shaw, and told that gentleman how Sir Alexander Midharst desired to see him with a view to making his will, and how the client, although in no immediate danger of death, was nevertheless in a state of health which made it highly desirable his worldly affairs should be put in order as quickly as possible.

Mr. Shaw visited the Castle that evening, wrote from the baronet's dictation, and on Monday, the 4th of June, 1866, the will was signed by Sir Alexander in the presence of two competent witnesses, who, in the presence of the testator and of one another, affixed their signatures.

A few days afterwards Mr. Gray met the lawyer.

"Well," said the banker, with one of

his easiest smiles, "did you do what was
required at the Castle ? "

"Yes," answered the white-haired solicitor, who was tremulous, and had a
disconcerting way of shutting his eyes and
consulting imaginary internal Acts of Parliament when he spoke. He was not by
nature communicative, and he held in rigid
regard all professional etiquette ; but Mr.
Henry Walter Grey was a very exceptional
man, and, moreover, the testator had told
him Mr. Grey had consented to act as
guardian and trustee ; therefore he did
not feel he committed any impropriety in
adding : " Sir Alexander appears to share
public feeling in your favour, and to place
unlimited confidence in our most careful
banker."

"You are very kind," returned Mr.
Grey, with his most cordial smile. "As
you know, our establishment has been a
long time connected with the Castle, and

when Sir Alexander asked me to act, it would look ungracious in me to refuse."

"It's a heavy responsibility."

"Oh, as far as the responsibility goes——" He did not finish the sentence in words, but with a shrug of his shoulders, as much as to say: "We bankers are accustomed to grave responsibilities." Then the two parted.

From this conversation Grey not only gathered that the will had been made, but also that under it he had been appointed executor and trustee to the document and the estate, and guardian to the heiress.

What more could he require to put his mind at rest?

And yet as the days went on he was far from easy. Many things caused him trouble and made him anxious. The gloom over the financial world deepened instead of lifting. The ordinary depositors grew shyer and shyer, as crash followed crash,

and house followed house, in the awful
ruin of the time.

No one breathed à word against the
Daneford Bank ; all who spoke of it
acknowledged its position unassailable ;
still its business showed no vast increase,
no such increase as would help Grey out
of the whirlpool into which he had been
drawn, although the Bank's borrowing
power had been secured.

From bad, things went to worse. As
the year wore on, some of his best customers began to feel the pressure of the
times. Instead of finding funds flowing
into the Bank in unexampled abundance,
money ran out.

Old respectable firms now came to him
and asked to be helped over the disastrous
period. They brought this security and
that, and begged for advances. If the
name and fame of the Bank were to be
magnified, this was the time to do it.

He had still funds enough to make the Bank proof against contingency; over and above this he had a little margin, not much, but most useful.

About the middle of June the Weeslade Steamship Company quarrelled with their bankers, the Weeslade Valley Bank. The Steamship Company wanted an advance of five thousand pounds on the river steamboat *Rodwell*, which carried passengers between Daneford and Seacliff. The Weeslade Valley Bank refused. The Steamship Company withdrew their account from the Valley Bank, and offered their business to the Daneford Bank. The account was opened in the Daneford, and the advance was made by mortgage on the *Rodwell*, the Steamship Company paying interest on the advance, and depositing with the mortgage a policy of insurance against total loss by water or weather.

Towards the end of June the Daneford

Bank's London agent failed, by which the Bank lost a clear twenty thousand pounds, besides losses by delay in getting a dividend. This was very serious. It caused a run on the Daneford Bank. In three days thirty thousand pounds were withdrawn in excess of average draughts.

On the morning of the third day the Daneford Bank issued a circular which took the town by storm. The circular was brief, and ran as follows :

"Thursday, 28th June, 1866.

"THE DANEFORD BANK.

"Take notice, owing to the fact that a run has begun on the Daneford Bank, the offices of that Bank will be opened every morning at eight instead of nine, and will be closed at seven instead of four p.m., until this run has ceased.

"HENRY WALTER GREY."

This circular was town talk the next

day. The admirers of Wat were more
enthusiastic than ever in their praises of
his boldness and wisdom. This circular
killed the panic, and on Saturday of
the same week the drawings had shrunk
back to an average. Yet for another
week the Bank was kept open from
eight in the morning till seven in the
evening.

On Monday, the 9th of July, a second
circular was issued from the Bank, saying
that as the run had ceased for a week the
office hours for the future would be as of
old, from 9 a.m. to 4 p.m.

But, although the run had ceased, upwards of thirty thousand pounds had been
withdrawn, and only five thousand found
its way back again, and that was decidedly
bad. The Bank was not in the least
jeopardy. Sir Alexander Midharst's half
a million had saved it; but the baronet's
money was not only not returning, but

the balance of it in hand began to run low.

Notwithstanding all this business pressure and the perilous position in which Grey stood, no one could detect in his face or manner a clue to the anxiety which consumed him. Still he was the same joyous companion, the same jovial host, the same considerate employer, the same liberal patron.

To his mother he displayed the best view of his position. He showed her how the steamship business had fallen in to him because he was in funds and could give accommodation beyond the power of his local rival. He admitted the loss in London, but pointed out how the loss and the run, taken together, must end in great advantage to his Bank.

She heard not only his story, but, from all who spoke to her on the subject, congratulations upon the Bank's position and his great prudence and good sense. He told her the money from Boston had not only saved him, but had so improved his resources that the Bank was now in fully as good a position as at any time during his father's lifetime.

Hard as the business affairs of Mr. Grey pressed upon him, and difficult as he felt the burden, they were not all the troubles he had to endure.

In order to prevent bankruptcy he had committed fraud. Up to this time he had carried on that fraud without exciting a hint of suspicion. The man whose money he had appropriated to his own use not only felt no misgivings as to the safety of his vast hoard, but had recently lavished upon him, Grey, the last proofs of implicit confidence when placing practically all that fortune and the care of the heiress in his hands.

But, as well as the pressure of his

business and the weight of his crime, he
had other difficulties to endure. He still
entertained his friends with his usual
hospitality and good grace, but the condition of the inner circle of his domestic
life grew daily harder and harder to bear.

The eccentricity of Mrs. Grey developed
with time, and, still more unfortunately,
the terrible infirmity to which she had
given way increased upon her with the
years.

She was childless; she was alone all
day in that great strange house; few
people called upon her, and she rarely
went out. Her husband was always kind
in manner towards her, and she could
ask for nothing he would not get her.
But she knew he and she were not one,
that they never had been one, that they
never could be one.

Mr. Grey did not lunch at home, so
that Mrs. Grey usually had luncheon by

herself, except upon the rare occasions
when one of her few acquaintances called
and stayed.

Seldom Mr. Grey dined out ; often
he had someone to dine with him, and
often he gave parties. All this caused
Mrs. Grey to be much by herself, and
solitude was, for one of her disposition
and tendency, fatal.

By little and little the disastrous
habit grew. It was most carefully concealed from the servants. At first Grey
had tried to effect a cure ; then, despair-
ing of that, he strove with all his skill
to avoid a scandal.

With that view he had a little cupboard
fitted up in the only room furnished in the
Tower. For this cupboard he got two
keys—one for himself, and one for his
wife. In giving her the key he had said
quietly :

" In future you will find the wine for

ordinary purposes in the new cupboard; so that you may not have the trouble of sending to the cellar for it, or in case I am out and you want more than is decanted, you can get it there. You will always have some there without sending to the cellar for it."

" But we don't want any more than is decanted—so few people call," said the wife tremulously.

" I know, I know. But someone may call, and as I keep the key of the cellar you might find yourself in a difficult position. Take this key of the cupboard, and here is the key of the room itself; there is only one other key, and I have that. The room is the quietest in the whole house. *The door locks on either the in or the outside.* The room is comfortably done up, and you can make any use you please of it. If you feel worried, or not very well, and wish to get away from the annoyance of the servants, you can go and lie down a while there."

These precautions were deplorable and degrading. All the love he had once borne this woman had died; and although he carefully concealed his feelings towards her, he had at last come to regard her with loathing.

She was in no way responsible for the disasters which had fallen on his business; she furnished no excuse for the crime he had committed, but she was one of the elements in his misfortune; and now that she had fallen into an odious fault, he resolved to put no impediment in her downward career, so long as her descent did not become apparent or public.

It was a sad development of the romantic and chivalric story of Wat Grey's wooing. But then, so long as Daneford knew nothing of the decay of that romance or the decline of that

chivalry, the fact that both were going—
gone, was of little moment to Wat Grey.

His embezzlement of the money had
taught him that damaging facts had no
injurious influence with the public—so
so long as the facts were carefully concealed. He found crime an easier burden
than he had expected, and in place of
his old dread of crime itself he had now
a dread of disclosure only. If he had
grown to hate his wife, what then—so
long as no one knew of it.

Up to this point Fate seemed to have
played deliberately into his hands. He
had ruined himself in Southern expecta-
tions, Fate had put more than half a
million of money into his power, and he
had extricated his fortune. An unlucky
turn of the die might have betrayed him,
and given him up to worse destruction
than the former, but all came round as
though he had the ordering of events.

Not only was there to be no immediate call for that money, no immediate investigation into accounts with a checking of documents and an examination of affairs, but he was appointed supreme custodian of the whole property, and, for upwards of a year from the old man's death, no enquiry disadvantageous to him could be set on foot.

Suppose the old man were to die soon, and business were to keep on the disastrous lines it had adopted of late ? What then?

What then ?

Many and many a day he put that question to himself in the morning before he broke his fast; and again at night before he went to bed he repeated this terrible question—unanswered.

And the more he pondered over this question the less he liked to look at the answer. Not that the simple and direct answer appalled him, for that had been familiar to his mind for some time; the simple answer was, Ruin—Self-imposed Death.

That was the positive answer to the question; but that did not affright him *now*, though it had terrified him at first.

He was still what might be called a young man, for he carried his five-and-forty years more easily than many another man carried thirty. He was not a whit insensible to the many physical and social personal advantages he possessed. He knew he was a favourite wherever he went. He knew he was good-looking. He knew he was clever.

He knew he was married.

His wife had brought him nothing worth speaking of—not position, happiness. He had been everything to her, and how poorly had she requited him! It was only by the utmost care he avoided a damning scandal alighting upon his name through her.

Fortune had favoured him up to this. Would Fortune be his friend still further? Was it too much to hope that another great piece of good luck might await him?

There was one sure way out of all his danger and difficulties, if he had only been a single man : there was Maud.

If, when Sir Alexander died, he were a bachelor, he might marry Maud. She knew nothing of the world, and he knew she liked him. There would be no need for his ruin if he were only a bachelor.

It was beyond the power of Fate to make him a bachelor; but suppose Fate should take away that unloved wife, that great danger to his name, that great stumbling-block in the way of his successful progress?

Then? What then? Answer: He

should marry Maud, and so wipe out the history of his crime.

Would chance or accident, would Heaven or Hell, or whatever else he might call it, take away from him this woman who was a curse and burden, and ·give him that woman who would bring him deliverance?

Such thoughts had long haunted his mind before he had heard on that 17th of August the voices which assailed and tempted him in tremendous tones; that day on which the fate of the steam-boat *Rodwell* and of Beatrice his wife, of the Weird Sisters and the Towers of Silence, became sealed together for ever.

CHAPTER IX.

A FLASK OF COGNAC.

WHEN the Weeslade Valley Bank declined to advance five thousand pounds on the Weeslade Steamship Company's river passenger-boat the *Rodwell*, they had two reasons for the refusal : first, they were not prepared to lock up money at the time ; second, a report reached them that the *Rodwell* was in bad condition.

In the winter of the year 1865 the *Rodwell* had lain up, undergoing repairs, and then the discovery was made that her condition was far from satisfactory. Many of her plates were no thicker than brown-paper, and just at the bends aft the point of a scraper had absolutely gone through a plate.

The boilers, too, were found to be in an unsatisfactory condition, and the machinery needed thorough overhauling.

But they wanted the boat for the summer traffic, and had no time to get all she required done before the fine weather; so she was patched for the time, the intention being to lay her up the following autumn and put her in good repair; in the meantime one new boiler was to be made for her.

Towards the middle of April she began running as usual with passengers between Daneford and Seacliff.

On her third trip she broke down; something went wrong with her machinery, and she had to be towed into Seacliff by another steamer.

As this accident occurred early in the season there were few passengers, and little excitement arose from the circumstance.

Almost the whole trade of the *Rodwell* consisted of carrying seaside folk from Daneford to Seacliff and back again. She sailed every week-day of the season from Seacliff to Daneford at half-past seven in the morning, and from Daneford to Seacliff at half-past six in the afternoon. Many of the business men of the city kept their families all the season at Seacliff, they themselves coming and going between the little town and the city daily, and enjoying the advantages of sleeping in sea-freshened air and two bright pleasant sails of a couple of hours each in the day.

When, in overhauling the *Rodwell* in 1865, they found the boilers in not a satisfactory condition, they took off five pounds of steam. "Better to be sure than sorry," they said. This reduction of steam made the *Rodwell* slower in 1866 than in previous years.

On Tuesday, the 14th of August, 1866, the engineer of the *Rodwell* made a report to the owners, and was directed to work her at another five pounds' reduction of pressure.

When Grey advanced the five thousand pounds on the mortgage he made no enquiry into her condition. He knew the boat very well, had many times travelled by her between Daneford and Seacliff. He knew she was worth more than the money asked for, and as no mortgage existed upon her he felt he should be quite secure if the company ensured her, and handed him a policy for five thousand pounds. His position was that if the company did not pay the interest on his money and his money itself, ultimately he could seize the *Rodwell*; and if the steamboat were lost by any chance of wind or water he

should get his money from the insurance
company.

Mr. Grey was as familiar with the
steamboat *Rodwell* as any man in Daneford. He had often spent the summer
months with his wife at Seacliff, and had
been a passenger in the boat hundreds
of times. He knew all the men employed
on her; he knew every exterior brass
plate and hinge and bolt. He could go
about her blindfold, and steer her up or
down the river. He didn't understand
machinery, but often said he could command, steer, and attend to the engines.
all by himself, and save the wages of the
crew.

Daneford was proud of all its institutions, and after Wat there were few it
felt more complaisant about than the
pretty town and picturesque scenery of
Seacliff and the faithful *Rodwell*, the town
being regarded as the country sweetheart,

the milkmaid lover of the city, and the steamboat as the Mercury of the love-making.

It was Grey's intention to spend the month of September, 1866, at Seacliff. He did not own a house there. It had been his custom to rent a small white cottage that hung half-way down a red cliff surrounding one of the blue bays clustering around the high headland on which the white town was built.

He did not regard his sojourn at Seacliff with any lively anticipations. It was pleasant to steam up and down the blue river between the sunlit green shores, through the sweet odours from the woods and hedges freshened and spiritualised by the full broad river. The morning swim in the strong sea-water brought the sense of health and vigour and power into his frame. The breakfast, ample, well cooked, appetising, with blithe company, full of inspiriting talk and resolute happiness, in the steamer's cabin, would cure a misanthrope and buoy the heart of a cynic. The joyous solemnity of that cigar on deck afterwards would reconcile an anchorite to comfort. Yet for all these advantages Henry Walter Grey did not like his season at Seacliff.

The evening voyage was no less to be enjoyed. After the dust and worry of the city's day it was good to feel the moist winds blowing through your hair, against your forehead; to hear the cooling swirl of the water at the bow, and the far-off wash of the steamer's swells upon the shadowy shore; to watch the crimson sunset, and the coming of the pale-blue stars, and the red moon that, slowly rising from the hot earth to the limpid sky, grew mild and fair, while under it the white earth sailed silent down the ocean of the dark; to feel the hallowed peace of night ascending from earth to God.

But it ruined all to know in that cottage above the bay on the ledge of red cliff one waited who was no companion, yet bound to him for life ; to know year by year the chasm between them widened ; and that above that chasm hung a spirit of evil, the bad angel of a terrible weakness, which might at any moment become visible to all those standing by, and ruin her, and bring on him pity — pity, that boneless scorn more unendurable than contempt or loathing.

In the deep seclusion of the Manor, Grey felt the skeleton in his house was pretty safely hidden ; here in Seacliff there were innumerable chances of discovery. It is more than likely he would not have gone to Seacliff in the summer if by any possibility he could safely avoid it. But all the well-off people of Daneford went

every year to the little town, and to
depart from the custom would be to attract
a dangerous attention to himself and his
household.   It had been his custom of
former years to stay at Seacliff for three
months of summer; but in the year 1866
he resolved to limit his stay to one month
—the month of September.

When he and she were at home in
the Manor House, she was more directly
under his control, immediately under his
observation.   But on leaving Seacliff in
the morning he was always weighed down
by the dread that in this little town of
much gossip something might leak out
while he was away.   She might go into
the town, and in some incautious way
betray her fault, and destroy all the
respect people felt for her—all the respect
they felt for his wife.

What an awful millstone to carry about
with one!   Fancy the men at the street-

corners chatting together, or groups standing
at the Chamber of Commerce windows, or
the members of the Club, or his own staff
at the Bank, looking after him with com-
passionate eyes, and saying : "Poor Wat !
How sad and worn and broken-down he
looks ! What a wretched thing ! What
a dreadful thing when a man's wife is
a—drunkard !"

The last word was always haunting
his ears, always booming in the hollow
caverns through which his fears followed
him during sleep ; and although the habit
of Mrs. Grey had not yet become so con-
firmed as to justify the application of
such an odious epithet, her case was
growing no better, growing rather worse
with time.

All the Midharst money was gone.
Her fault was at most a vice ; but he
had committed a crime. He lay between
two fears ; he was threatened by two

discoveries. Someone might find out about her, and blast the fame of the Manor House ; someone might find out about him, and blast the Daneford Bank, and lock him up in jail, and brand the name he bore with ignominy.

In such a state of mind was Grey when the 16th of August arrived and evening brought him home. The husband and wife sat down alone to dinner, sat down alone to the last dinner they were ever to eat together.

"Bee," said Grey to his wife, when the dessert had been brought in and the servants had gone, " do you think you could go down to Seacliff in the *Rodwell* to-morrow evening, and look up the cottage ? I saw the estimable and penurious landlord of it to-day. It's not occupied this month, and he wanted me to take it from the 20th. I'm half inclined to accept his offer. He says we can have it from the 20th of this month to the end of September for a month's rent. It would be almost worth while to take him at his word, and hear how he'd whine if I gave him a cheque for the month's rent only. What are those two famous items out of last year's bill?"

"Brunswick varnish, for the kitchen coal-scuttle, 2*d.*; and a pair of brass stair-eyes, one lost and one damaged, 2*d.*," quoted Mrs. Grey seriously, as if the imposition was intolerable.

"Yes, yes. That's it. Brunswick varnish and stair - eyes," laughed Grey. "And at the end of all the items for damage was the general observation: 'The same being in excess of reasonable wear and tear.' Didn't he make us whiten all the ceilings, too, on the grounds that we stopped far into the season and blackened them with the lamps?"

" Yes, Wat."

" Is it three or four times we have paid, Bee, for cracking that soup-tureen ? The old crack, you know."

" We've paid, I think, Wat, only twice for that crack, but he has charged us with the ladle every year, although we never had one."

" Why, this old Parkinson is much more amusing than a state-jester of old, and not half so impudent or expensive." Mr. Grey smiled, and rubbed his smooth cheek with his white hand. After a moment's enjoyment of his recollections of Parkinson, he returned to the question. " Well, Bee, will you go down in the *Rodwell* with me to-morrow evening ? We can have a breath of sea-air, a look at Parkinson and the cottage, and come back by the boat in the morning."

" Very well, Wat. Of course I'll go with you."

" Now let me see. The best plan will be for you to go from this to the boat. Be on board at a quarter-past six, and stay there until I come. You won't forget ? "

" No, Wat."

" You're quite sure you won't forget ? " Of late Mrs. Grey's memory had shown signs of giving way.

" I'll be there, certainly," she answered, a little hotly. " You don't think my memory is so bad I am likely to forget anything that gives me a chance of getting out of this dull house."

" Because," he said, holding up his finger to quiet her displeasure, " I may not be able to get away from the office until just half-past six. I shall be at the boat in time. You will go aboard and sit down aft, and wait for me."

Having thus arranged for the following evening, Grey lapsed into silence, and his wife withdrew.

Those after-dinner hours, which, to the prosperous man are the most placid and full of content, were now to Grey full of fears and subtle agonies when he had no company. The necessity all through the day for showing a fair front to the world and keeping up his reputation for cordial joviality no longer existed when he found himself alone in his own dining-room.

Then he exposed his imagination to all the dangers and difficulties in his path. Here, this 16th of August, was he safe over all the wreck of that awful month of May, but at what a cost? The commission of a disgraceful crime and the perpetual dread of a damning discovery.

The financial crisis had shattered trade, dispersed confidence, and ruined enterprise. The last penny of the baronet's money had been taken, and was gone; and yet no remarkable prosperity, nothing in the meanest way approaching what he

had calculated upon, had set in towards
him. Even in the recent days of over-
trading, when money was dear, the deposits
in the Daneford Bank had been more than
during the past few months. Things were
not likely to mend in time for him. At
the present rate twenty years could not
bring in half the sum he wanted, and he
might be called to disgorge within eighteen
months, within a much less time should
the old baronet suddenly die and matters
take a turn unfavourable to his interest
with regard to the guardianship of the
heiress—his care over her not reaching,
he supposed, beyond her twenty-first
birthday. Merciful Heavens! what could
deliver him?

And then followed the invariable
reply: There is nothing to save you
from infamy but marriage with Maud
Midharst.

Then the memory of his wife's faults

came up before him like an indictment seeking her life. She was flighty, unwise, dull, uncompanionable—intemperate.

She was no pleasure to him. She seemed to be the source of no pleasure to herself. If the Powers of good would only take her, what a blessed relief to him!

If the Powers of any denomination whatever would only take her and leave him free!

He rose, and strode up and down the long room, his face puckered and pinched, his hands clutched, his eyebrows dragged down over his eyes until the eyes disappeared, those eyes wont to be so free and open.

If the Powers of any denomination whatever—— His thoughts paused a while, his brows relaxed, his whole face changed character, put on holiday attire. With a light foot and a pleasant smile he approached the chimney-piece and pulled the bell.

"James," he said, when the man entered, "bring me a flask of cognac."

While the servant was going to the cellar he said to himself, with a gentle smile, "I have been very thoughtless about that press in the Tower of Silence. I have left claret and port and sherry there, but until now I never remembered brandy! How careless I have been."

In a few minutes James returned with the bottle, drew the cork, decanted the brandy, and left.

Grey took up the decanter with a cordial smile on his face, walked towards the tower-room, the first-floor room in the Tower of Silence upon the top of which the wasted skeleton of the huge tank stood out clear against the quiet summer stars.

It was now past eleven o'clock. No

profounder silence reigned by night in
deserted mine deep in the bowels of the
earth, in Asian desert open to the
glittering stars and the pale radiance of
the moon, on the dark peaks of mighty
alp that reaches upward into the thin
windless air, than in the chambers and
passages of the fearful Manor House.

As he draws near the door of the
tower-room he carries the decanter of
brandy in one hand, a lighted candle in
the other. When only a few feet separate
him from the door he pauses suddenly,
and looks earnestly forward. There are
two keys for that door, one is on his
ring, the other is in the possession of his
wife. He holds the lamp high above his
head, and listens intently. Yes; there
is someone inside.

While he waits he hears a lock shot.
Presently the door opens, and with a cry
of surprise and fear his wife confronts him.

"Bee," he says, without allowing the smile to relax, "is this you? I thought you were gone to bed."

"I went to my room," says the unhappy woman, trembling and looking down, "but I could not sleep. I was very nervous and—and, Wat, I thought a glass of port might do me good."

"Of course it will. Of course it will," he says, in a soft voice. "I was just going to put this in the cupboard." He holds up the decanter.

"What is that?" she asks, in a voice full of uneasiness and fear.

"Only a little brandy. It's not a rattle-snake or a petard that you need be afraid of, Bee," he replies, in a bantering tone.

"No, no, Wat," she cries, drawing back a pace and holding up her hands as though she saw some fearful object in her way. "We don't want any brandy here. Indeed we don't."

" What nonsense !" he laughs. " But, seriously, Bee, you know we must have some brandy here. Suppose one of the servants, or any chance caller were to become suddenly faint, what could you do without brandy ? "

" Don't put it there, Wat! For my sake, for God's sake, don't put it there ?" She covers her face with her hands, and trembles again.

" There now, Bee, go to bed, and don't be silly. I should never be able to forgive myself if any harm came of there being no brandy that could be readily got at."

With slow heavy steps the woman passes him, and, as she reaches the end of the short corridor, throws up her hands to heaven, sobs out, "God be merciful to me!" and bursts into tears.

He waits until she is out of the passage, then shrugs his shoulders, and, with the old, genial smile upon his face deposits

the decanter of cognac in the cupboard
of the room on the first floor of the
tower, of that tower which, in a moment
of grim humour, he had called the Tower
of Silence.

CHAPTER X.

MR. GREY breakfasted early, Mrs. Grey late. Nothing was said by either to the other on the night of the 16th. On Friday morning, the morning of the 17th of August, 1866, Mrs. Grey was still sleeping when her husband left the house.

The morning was bright and clear, and as the banker strode on briskly to the city he hummed an air to keep him company. His voice was indifferent, his ear was indifferent, and yet it was more invigorating to hear him blundering out wild approximations to a tune than to listen to a moderately accomplished drawing-room vocalist. The banker seemed unable to keep the natural gladness of his nature within bounds; the accomplished vocalist follows an every-day handicraft or trade with the tools of which he is familiar and expert.

As Grey walked to his office that bright Friday morning he met many friends and acquaintances. He had a nod, a wave of the hand, a cheerful word, a kind enquiry, a jovial wish, a congratulation for each, according to person and circumstances.

He carried his black bag in his hand. In the black bag were some books, some papers, and the revolver. Nothing particular occurred to him on the way to the Bank. Nothing particular awaited him upon his arrival at the office. All was going on smoothly and prosperously —but very slowly, very slowly towards bringing back the baronet's money.

Two was his luncheon hour, and at

two he went out. He lunched at his club, and then strolled down to the Chamber of Commerce to see the latest Exchange telegrams, and have a chat with some of the merchants and traders and shipowners of Daneford. He got back to the office at a little after three.

Nothing particular had occurred during his absence. He went into his private room and disposed of some routine affairs. Then, having no business to do, he threw up the window, and looking out, began to whistle softly a recitative of his own invention.

After a little while he stopped whistling, and thought: "I shall be here two hours by myself this evening. I don't think I could do anything better than burn that book." In a little while more he made up his mind. "Yes; I will burn it. It would tell against me in any case. Even suppose by any miracle I am able to get

that money together again, the dates
would betray me. Then it is better to
have neither book nor Stock than a tell-
tale book only. Dead men and burnt
books tell no tales. Yes; up the chimney
it shall go. If I am able to replace that
money, the making of a new book will
be an easy task, a graceful amusement."

Mr. Grey had always kept the Midhurst
(Consols) account in his own handwriting,
and in a book to which none but himself
had access. This was a small book bound
in rough calf, having a patent lock and
key. Before the Bank closed at four
o'clock he went down to the strong-room
and took up this book to his private
office.

By about half-past four all the clerks
had left the office, and Mr. Aldridge had
gone out to pick up an appetite for dinner.
Grey locked the two doors that led into
his office, opened the little ledger, and

having cut the book out of the cover, he
locked up the cover in a safe in the wall
of his own office. There were two reasons
for doing this : 1. The cover was, with
the appliances at his command, indestruc-
tible. 2. He could get new paper bound
into the old cover; and those of his staff
who were familiar with the outside of the
book would not be able to detect any
difference between the original and the
counterfeit.

When the cover of the book had been
concealed under lock and key he sat down
in front of the grate, and began tearing
up the book into single leaves, and
burning each one separately in the empty
grate.

As the record of the baronet's twenty
years of grinding, exaction, and penurious
living changed into flame and smoke and
ashes, Grey's thoughts were busy with the
awful aspects of his position, and now,

for the first time, a new element of fear
entered into the case.

He suddenly stopped in his work and
looked round him with a ghastly smile.
Last night he had been calculating
that his only way of avoiding exposure
lay through the freedom of himself to
marry Maud. But suppose anything were
to happen to his wife *now*. Suppose she
died that very day; suppose she had died
a week ago, a month ago; what would
have occurred? He should then be a
childless widower, younger in appearance
and in manner than in years, and even
young enough in years to be the suitor
of any girl. Was it likely if he were
so circumstanced Sir Alexander might not
think of altering the will, of introducing
into it another guardian, executor, or
trustee? True, Sir Alexander was not an
ordinary man, and had unlimited confidence in him, Grey; but surely he could

not be such a fool as to leave his daughter
and his daughter's fortune in the hands
solely of a popular, good-looking, and
an agreeable widower of forty-five?

The thought flurried him, and he
gasped and covered his face with his
handkerchief, and leaned upon the mantel-
piece.

Last night it had appeared to him
nothing more advantageous to his fortune
could arise than the death of his wife.
Now that event seemed the most disastrous which could befall him. The more
he looked at the whole situation the more
hopeless his position appeared. What last
night he regarded as the gateway to
deliverance now was the cavern of ruin.
Well, he had begun burning this book.
and he might as well finish it. Destroying
this could have no important influence
for evil on the case, and might be bene-
ficial or have a mitigating influence.

At last the whole book lay in a mass of black and blue ashes at his feet. He stood in front of the pile for a few moments thinking. "Between that book and me there is great similarity. It was once truthful, then it recorded a lie, and now it is burnt and black. I was once honest; I fell; and now my position, my prospects, and my hopes are in ashes. There is no chance of escape."

It was after five o'clock. He rang the bell; as he did so, he heard the street-bell ring also.

"Aldridge coming back from his constitutional." Then, correcting himself, he thought: "Of course, Aldridge doesn't ring."

He unlocked the doors, and in a few minutes the servant knocked and entered.

"I want you to tidy up that grate; I've been burning some old letters," said Grey.

"Yes, sir; a letter for you, sir, just come."

"All right; leave it on my table."

"Beg pardon, sir, but it's from the Castle, and marked immediate."

The banker took it and glanced at the superscription as the servant withdrew.

"From Mrs. Grant," he muttered. "What can it be now?"

He tore open the envelope and read the contents hastily. The note was very brief. Sir Alexander had had a bad night, and was rather worse this morning. He particularly wanted to see Mr. Grey *at once.* Would Mr. Grey be so good as to come *instantly* upon receipt of this? The words in italics were underlined heavily three or four times.

"What can this be?" he thought. "The last time I got a note from Mrs. Grant asking me to go to the Castle I was in the final extremity of apprehension, and all came much better than I could have dared to hope. There seems no possibility of a favourable solution of the present situation. If the old man is sinking, that will give me only a year—and that is the least terrible thing can cause this hasty summons. Well, go I must, and at once."

He leaped lightly down the stairs, carrying his bag in his hand, and was soon driving rapidly towards Island Ferry.

Two miles lay between him and the city before he remembered his appointment with his wife on board the *Rodwell*.

"Never mind," he thought, "I'll board the steamboat as she passes the Island; that will make it all right."

By six o'clock he had reached Island Ferry. Without the loss of a moment he crossed over to the Island and ascended towards the Castle.

A servant at once conducted him to

Mrs. Grant, who was waiting for him in the hall-room off the grand entrance-hall.

"O Mr. Grey, I am so glad you have come; we are in such fearful anxiety. Poor Sir Alexander has got worse and worse ever since I wrote to you. The doctors say this is what they have been dreading all along."

The little woman was in a state of the greatest excitement, and had completely lost all sense of proportion. The standards of her feelings had been broken by her agitation, and everything that went wrong seemed of equal importance and mischief.

"What is the matter now?" the banker asked, in a soft sympathetic voice. "I hope Miss Midharst," he added, before he gave the little widow time to answer, "is kept as free as possible from these sad and depressing scenes.

"Oh, yes; that is, I mean the poor

child is fearfully distressed. She has been with her father all day. It's not good for her, but then she wouldn't come away. I think if you spoke to her it would do her good. She used to mind a good deal what I said to her, but all this day she sits there, staring as if the room was full of ghosts. I fear there's something bad the matter with the whole place; and only for darling Maud, I'm sure I shouldn't stop an hour. And to listen to him is something dreadful. He talks of nothing but his money and you and robbery——"

"What!" exclaimed Grey, loudly and sharply.

"Now," she cried, "you are offended with me just because I am nervous and excitable. Maybe *you'd* be excited yourself, Mr. Grey, if he was turning to you every minute and saying you were a wolf in sheep's clothing, and that you wanted to rob his child of the fortune he had laid by for her. You wouldn't like to be called a robber, and you're a man, and I am only a nervous woman; and men are more used to that kind of language than women, although, until now, I did not know that gentlemen ever used such words."

Here Mrs. Grant broke down completely, and sobbed.

By this time Grey had recovered from the appalling shock caused by Mrs. Grant's association of himself with theft. He went up to the sobbing woman, and in his gentlest accents, having placed his hand reassuringly on her shoulder, said:

"Mrs. Grant, I am exceedingly sorry if my hasty exclamation has caused you any annoyance. Believe me, nothing was further from my intention than to disturb you under the distressing circumstance you describe, and in the very shattered condition in which your nerves must be.

Forgive me, pray. Do say that you forgive me."

He pleaded in his most winning voice and manner; he looked upon the friendliness of Mrs. Grant towards him as of great importance.

"It wasn't your fault, Mr. Grey," said Mrs. Grant, quieting her sobs. "I know I am not fit for anything of this kind; it always knocks me up."

"No wonder. Of course, as you say, such expressions are never heard among gentlemen——"

She interrupted him.

"I hope I didn't say anything unbecoming to you; if I did, I didn't mean it. I am so worried and confused I don't know what I'm saying." By this time she had forgotten the cause of her tears. What Grey said made her believe she herself had uttered something offensive to the banker. "I wonder can it be that

I have caught the fever from Sir Alexander, and am not in my right mind ?"

"No, no, no," laughed Grey reassuringly. "You need not be afraid of that." He had no desire to recall to her memory the words which had drawn from him the abrupt and disconcerting exclamation. "And so," he said, in a bland voice, "poor Sir Alexander's head is wandering."

"Oh, yes. He began to be queer last night, and got worse all the night. This morning we sent for the doctors, and they came again in the afternoon. At the latter visit they said I had better send for you, as you were so much in Sir Alexander's mind, both when he was raving and when he wasn't."

"Then he has lucid intervals ?"

"Oh, yes—or, at least, not quite lucid. There are times when he is less wild than others ; but I think his mind is not quite free at any time. I have been keeping you here instead of taking you direct to him, as I should have done. You will excuse me; my poor head is quite gone too. Will you come with me to him now ?"

"Yes," he answered, with a profound bow.

As he followed her through the dull stately passages that, although it was still full daylight, were dim and funereal, he tried to pierce the veil of the future. How would this sudden development of the old man's disease affect him? Was the old man in his comparatively lucid moments capable of altering his will? What was the cause of the old man's desire to see him? And, above all, how had this idea of theft come upon him?

So far as he could now form an opinion of the case, he did not feel reassured.

Suppose Mrs. Grant's account of the

baronet's condition of mind in the less
excited moments was overdrawn, and that
while in his periods of delirium he was
haunted by goblin fears of robbers, in
his more collected phases he might be
troubled with reasonable dread of theft
or misappropriation or fraud. Did the
old man desire to destroy or alter his
will? That was the vital question. If
he did, then surely the lead would overtake the gold.

The gold! That gold could never be
won back, not in as many years as it
took the baronet to save it up. Not in
twice as many years, and he might have
no more than one year. The gold could
never overtake the lead now—that is,
the gold, the Consols.

But the gold of a wedding-ring for
Miss Midharst would balance the five-tons
weight of the baronet's. Little over half
an ounce of gold would outweigh five

tons ; a ring that cost no more than three
guineas would balance a deficit of five
hundred and fifty thousand pounds !

Mrs. Grant softly opened the door of
the sick chamber, and motioning someone
inside to come near, she said, as Miss
Midharst approached :

" Maud, dear, here is Mr. Grey ; he
came at once."

The girl offered him her hand, and Grey
took it respectfully, tenderly, and held it,
saying :

" I am deeply grieved, Miss Midharst,
at what Mrs. Grant tells me. I hope this
may be only a temporary affection. How
is Sir Alexander now ? "

" Oh, he's very, very bad ! " sobbed
the girl, in a whisper. " It was kind
of you to come. He talks of you
always."

" I am, believe me, Miss Midharst,
deeply grieved for him, and—you."

Nothing could be more kind and sympathetic than his voice and manner.

"He talks of nothing but you and the money," whispered the girl, through her tears.

At that moment a shrill shout came from the bed, followed by the words:

"Ah, Grey, is that you? You thieving scoundrel! Do you dare to come into my house, under my roof, after stealing my darling's fortune! Bring me my pistols, I say—some one bring me my pistols! I will shoot this miscreant banker Grey. My pistols, I say!"

CHAPTER XI.

For a moment Grey paused irresolutely on the threshold of the sick room. This was the most alarming ordeal to which he had been subjected. Could it be that by any untoward circumstance of disastrous fate the old man had discovered the truth?

To be loudly, violently accused of the crime he had committed by the man whose money he had stolen, and in the presence of that man's daughter!

He had often in his worst moments imagined the position he now occupied, but had never dared to think of, it had never entered his moments of wildest fear to realise, such a scene conducted in the presence of Miss Midharst and Mrs. Grant. And now to the horrors of hearing such words from the defrauded man's lips, was added the awful question, the appalling uncertainty in the questions: Did the baronet know anything? Did he know all?

His name for honour, for honesty, the existence of the respectable old institution which had been handed down to him by his father unsullied, his very life, hung upon these two questions. There was only one chance between him and ruin, between him and death. At these thoughts he made a prodigious effort, and turning to the two distracted woman with a forced smile, and a lip he could not keep from trembling, said:

"I fear my presence only excites Sir Alexander. Had I not better retire until he is more calm?"

" Oh, Mr. Grey," said Maud through her tears, "you must not mind his words. He does not know what he says. He does not understand what is said to him. He does not even know who is in the room when he is in this state. My poor father, oh, my poor father!" She covered her face with her hands and sobbed out.

Grey began to breathe more freely. He whispered, as though the weight of a mountain were rolling off him, "He does not know what he says. He does not know who is in the room. Poor gentleman! Poor Sir Alexander! I am profoundly sorry for him and for you, Miss Midharst. You can understand how much I was surprised to hear him, who has so long relied upon me, use such words to me. It was, you must admit," he looked from the woman to the girl in deferential appeal, "rather startling."

" We know what he thinks of you

when he is in his right senses, Mr. Grey," said Mrs. Grant. "We know he has the greatest confidence in you."

The banker bowed deeply, and when he had straightened himself once more, regarded the widow with profound and sorrowful attention.

Mrs. Grant continued: "In his lucid moments he asked for you, and seemed anxious to see you on business, as of old; but when he raved as he did just now, he accused us all of taking his money."

"What a sad and distracting form of delusion!" murmured the banker. He could scarcely contain himself. He would at that moment have forfeited the five thousand pounds advanced on the mortgage of the *Rodwell* if he might throw his arms into the air and shout out and laugh and dance.

The sick man spoke of everyone as a thief in his frenzy, but in his clear

moments spoke of him, Grey, as of old !
He did not suspect him exclusively; the
indictment to which he had listened in
paralysed terror had been by accident
preferred against him; by accident it
might have been preferred against any
other human being with whose name Sir
Alexander was familiar !

The weight of earth had rolled back
from his breast, and he was breathing
more freely than for many a long day.

The three now left the door and walked
into the room. At best the vast chamber
was gloomy, but now all light but a
faint dim glow that clung to the inside
of the curtains was excluded.

Grey placed himself at the side of
the vast bedstead. Sir Alexander had
sold off all his personal furniture; he
occupied one of the state rooms and slept
in one of the enormous state bedsteads;
these bedsteads were in the deeds he

could not alter, and had to go down to
the next heir. The first look the banker
cast at the face of the sick man gave him
a shock.

The old baronet had always had a
colour in his cheeks; now all the colour
was gone from the cheeks and gathered
into the temples and forehead. The
wrinkled forehead was of a dull brick
colour. The great forked dark vein of
the forehead stood up out of the dry red
skin like the forked mullion of a gothic
window, against whose crimson panes the
west is red. In the temples of the old
man the rugged veins were swollen and
knotted, and in the purple hollows between
the dark blue knots a quick feeble pulse
fluttered and hurried forward like a
frightened hunted beast. Through the
counterpane the thin form showed sharply.
The breathing was quick and unquiet,
the eyes staring and fixed upon the carved

oak ceiling. Apparently the delirious paroxysm had passed, and the patient was suffering from modified collapse.

"He will be better presently, and may recognise you," whispered Mrs. Grant into Grey's ear. She stood by his side. At the foot stood Maud, weeping softly, silently. For a while no one moved.

Gradually the breathing of the sick man grew more steady, and the fluttering pulse in the hollow temples more regular.

"In a few minutes," whispered the widow, "he will be quite collected."

As she had foretold, his eyes descended from the ceiling and began running over the room and those present, as if trying to recover memory. At length they were fixed on Grey and did not move from him. Although the eye was dull and clouded, there was a look of intelligence in it. It was the eye of a weakened intellect rather than of a disordered one.

"Ah, Grey, is that you?"

"Yes, Sir Alexander. I hope you feel better?"

"I am quite well. I have been greatly troubled about that money, those Consols. They tell me they have been sold. Is it true that my Consols have been sold? I ask you in the presence of my daughter, for whom they were saved, have they been sold?" The sick man's eyes were filmy; but while they were dull to the perception of surrounding objects, they seemed to be partly closed against objects of natural vision only that they might be partly opened to unascertainable forms and figures of supernatural view.

Grey's heart quailed. Who were "they" that had informed him of the fraud? What did the sick man know of the fraud? What did he surmise? Was there anything but imagination to account for these fears, these hideous questions, this awful ordeal ? He was sorry he had left his bag below in the little room where Mrs. Grant had received him. Nothing could save him now but a calm exterior and intrepid audacity. He cleared his throat to make sure his voice was obedient to his will, and answered boldly, but softly :

"No one has sold the Consols, Sir Alexander. I answer you faithfully, in your presence and in the presence of Miss Midharst, for whose benefit they have been acquired and put by."

He was amazed himself at the firmness and clearness of his voice. If it had been merely repeating the words of another man, his voice could not have been less open to suspicion ; if he had been pronouncing a most consoling truth, his manner could not have been more benignly reassuring. Instead of the words being those of another, they were so

intimately his own that his existence
depended upon their utterance ; instead
of being true, they contained a lie so
monstrous under the circumstances that
they were as false and wicked as a blas-
phemous false oath.   He thought to himself
grimly, as he rapidly reviewed the words
and the import of his voice : " I am acting
in a play of the Devil's writing, and must
do honour to the character I represent
and credit to the author."

The eyes of the old man were fixed
on the banker's face as he said : " What
you tell me of my money, *her* money, is
quite true ?   It is quite safe ?   No one
has sold out ?"

" It is quite true ; no one has sold
out."

" Swear it !"

" I swear it."

" Mrs. Grant, get the Book.   I am a
magistrate, and you shall swear the formal

oath, so that you may be punished if you are hiding the truth from an old helpless man."

Mrs. Grant placed a Testament on the bed beside Mr. Grey. The latter took up the Book. He did not care to question the legality of such an oath. He thought he would humour the old man. A crime or two more were nothing to him now, particularly when these crimes helped to cover up the other crime of embezzlement, theft, fraud—call it what you will.

Mr. Grey took up the Testament, and Sir Alexander, in a confused way, repeated words which could not be clearly heard, but ended with the clause usual to the ending of a formal oath.

Mr. Grey kissed the Book reverentially, and murmured the final words. As he uttered the words, he could not avoid the reflection that if he were acting in a play of the Devil's writing, some of the words to be uttered had a peculiar aspect as coming from the Master of Evil.

Mr. Grey put the Book on the bed, and looked with reassuring glance at both the women. The old baronet muttered to himself indistinctly for a few seconds. "Bad dreams, bad dreams," he said distinctly at last; "they were only dreams."

Mr. Grey looked round again at the women and inclined his head significantly to them, as though he would say : "Poor Sir Alexander ! His dreams must have been bad indeed, if he fancied anyone had taken his money."

By this the great flush had disappeared from the old man's forehead, the veins had subsided, and a deadly pallor covered his features from forehead to chin. During the paroxysms of his delirium, it seemed as though his head was in danger of bursting from too great a supply of heated blood ; now it looked as if the

walls of his skull and the flesh of his
face were about to crumble and fall in
for want of fluid sufficient to sustain
their weight. But in the eye still lingered
the heat and flickered the fire of the fever.
He lay still for a while, and seemed to be
about to fall asleep. Presently, however,
all were startled to hear his voice ring
out clear and firm, high above their
notion of his present strength, clear above
their notion of his intellectual capacity :

"Henry Grey, take her hand, my
daughter's hand, and lead her here—no
the other hand—give her your left hand,
Henry Grey."

Mr. Grey walked to where the girl
stood, now pale and tearless, at the foot
of the bed, and offered her his right
hand ; then his left, and led her to the
side of the bed, where he had been
standing.

"Now, Henry Grey, take the Testament

in your right hand. I am going to make you swear—I am a deputy-lieutenant—to guard with all your power and wiles, my only daughter, Maud Midharst, herself and her fortune and her happiness. Say the words after me."

"Herself and her fortune and her happiness to guard with all my power," he repeated.

"All your power and wiles," insisted the old man, in a tone of exasperation.

"My power and—wiles," repeated Mr. Grey, after a slight hesitation.

"To act as executor of my will, trustee to her fortune, and guardian of my child. So help me, God."

Mr. Grey repeated the words with solemn deliberation.

"Kiss the Book."

Mr. Grey bent his head reverentially over the sacred volume and kissed it devoutly.

"Kiss the Book, my child. Take it in your own right hand and kiss it. It is the history of the life and sufferings and death of our Lord, and something of great moment is conducting."

"Kiss the Book, you also," looking towards Mrs. Grant.

She did as he desired.

"Now, my daughter, and you, Henry Grey, both together hold that Book, which is the history of the life and sufferings and death of our Lord, to my lips, for I am weak and unable, and I will kiss it last of all."

They placed the Book against his lips, and when he had kissed it they drew it back, and placed the Testament on the bed.

Mr. Grey folded his arms tightly across his chest; he had a feeling that his chest would burst if he did not shout out and relieve it.

"My daughter," said the sick man, "if I should never get off this bed again—and I feel that something great is conducting—when I am dead you will look to him for all advice and guidance. He will be your friend, your only friend, who can be of aid to you when I am dead. You will lean upon him. He will guard your money and see that no one does you ill or cheats you. He is an honest man, Maud. He has taken care of your fortune for me until now; he will take care of it for you when I am dead. You will have no one else but him; no friend in all the world but Henry Grey."

"Oh, my God!" burst from the banker. If the hangman were in the room, and any word spoken by him, Grey, was to be the signal for his death, he could not restrain himself.

For a moment they all three looked at him in grave surprise. His words were not perhaps improper to the grave occasion, but his manner of uttering them had something startling in it. There was in his tone a cry of wild appeal against an inexorable decree of prodigious woe. His voice had more the sound of a brute's inarticulate cry of despair than any human agony fitted to human words. It was a death-cry, the death-cry of some fine instinct of the human soul. It was a cry the like of which no man utters twice in a lifetime.

The old man regarded the banker for a moment with a look of surprise. Then the expression of the old man's face softened, and he said : "Grey, my arm is weak. I cannot raise it. Take my hand. You will be good to her when I am dead. I know what the world may say. It may say, Grey, that you and I are not equals ; that I might have bestowed the guardianship of my daughter's fortune among houses such as the Fleureys' or the Midharsts'. But I know what you are and what your father was, and I am placing what I value above all earthly things in your keeping. I am an old man, and the doctors may be right this time. I am old and weak, Henry Grey, and I want you to be her friend when I am dead. The world may say what it pleases about you as guardian. I am firm in my faith in you. No orphan, friendless—the last, I may say, of her house—had ever a more careful or prudent or wise guardian than you. I am old and weak. There is one more favour I would ask of you before you go—for I have said all. You will not refuse an old man on his death-bed, Henry Grey?"

"No," in a faint thin whisper.

"I am weak, and cannot do it myself. Raise up my hand held in yours, and place your hand against my lips, that I

may kiss the hand which is to shield my
daughter when I am gone."

"Oh, Sir Alexander!" in a tone of
agonized protest.

"I am very old and very weak. You
will not, because I am old and weak
and cannot raise your hand, deny me
this pleasure."

The banker did as he was asked.

When he had placed the cold thin
hand back again on the bed, the baronet
sighed and murmured: "I am tired.
I will try to sleep awhile. You may go,
Henry Grey. God bless you, Henry Grey!
Now I am at rest!"

With a deep bow to the ladies, Mr.
Grey left the room. He went down a
passage and then turned into another.
Here he was alone, out of sight and
earshot. He threw his arms heavily up,
straight above his head, and flung himself
against the wall with a groan, beat his

arms and hands against the wall, and struck his forehead against the wall.

"Do I live?" he cried; "or am I already among the damned?"

END OF VOL. I.

CHARLES DICKENS AND EVANS, GREAT NEW STREET, FETTER LANE, E.C